SPECIAL MESSAGE TO READERS

THE ULVERSCROFT FOUNDATION
(registered UK charity number 264873)

was established in 1972 to provide funds for research, diagnosis and treatment of eye diseases. Examples of major projects funded by the Ulverscroft Foundation are:-

- The Children's Eye Unit at Moorfields Eye Hospital, London
- The Ulverscroft Children's Eye Unit at Great Ormond Street Hospital for Sick Children
- Funding research into eye diseases and treatment at the Department of Ophthalmology, University of Leicester
- The Ulverscroft Vision Research Group, Institute of Child Health
- Twin operating theatres at the Western Ophthalmic Hospital, London
- The Chair of Ophthalmology at the Royal Australian College of Ophthalmologists

You can help further the work of the Foundation by making a donation or leaving a legacy. Every contribution is gratefully received. If you would like to help support the Foundation or require further information, please contact:

THE ULVERSCROFT FOUNDATION
The Green, Bradgate Road, Anstey
Leicester LE7 7FU, England
Tel: (0116) 236 4325
website: www.foundation.ulverscroft.com

WATSON'S LOST DISPATCH BOX

Thomas Jones, a retired professor of English and rare book dealer, is astounded when a young man enters his shop offering an almost pristine copy of *The Strand Magazine* from July 1891, containing the Sherlock Holmes story *A Scandal in Bohemia*. But what shocks Thomas the most is that below the magazine title is a stamped inscription proclaiming in large block letters 'AUTHOR COPY'. Thus begins an astonishing adventure leading to murder — both past and present — and the discovery of Dr. John H. Watson's lost dispatch box!

Books by Gary Lovisi
in the Linford Mystery Library:

SHERLOCK HOLMES AND THE
CROSBY MURDERS
THE SECRET FILES OF
SHERLOCK HOLMES
MURDER OF A BOOKSELLER
THE PLOT AGAINST
SHERLOCK HOLMES
SHERLOCK HOLMES AND MR. MAC
MORE SECRET FILES OF
SHERLOCK HOLMES

GARY LOVISI

WATSON'S LOST DISPATCH BOX

Complete and Unabridged

LINFORD
Leicester

First published in Great Britain

First Linford Edition
published 2018

A catalogue record for this book is available from the British Library.

ISBN 978–1–4448–3564–9

Published by
F. A. Thorpe (Publishing)
Anstey, Leicestershire

Set by Words & Graphics Ltd.
Anstey, Leicestershire
Printed and bound in Great Britain by
T. J. International Ltd., Padstow, Cornwall

This book is printed on acid-free paper

1

A Mystery in Dorchester

It was another quiet day at The Rare Book Shoppe, the out-of-print specialty bookstore that I now own in my retirement years, set on a trendy street in the small New England town of Dorchester. Being a book lover all my life, as well as a collector of same, it just seemed natural that upon my retirement as a local college English professor, I would embark upon my new dream career, that of owning a bookstore.

Of course, it was not at all what I thought it would be.

I do find bookselling an interesting and even enjoyable pastime. The store helps to pay my rent and expenses — though in truth my pension from a very generous local college really keeps me flush with cash. Still and all, I do love my little bookstore — even if most people don't seem to read anymore. But what the heck, I'm a sixty-two-year-old widower who hasn't anything much better to do with his time these days. I didn't expect to have too much of that left either, at the rate I was going, with various illnesses I'll not bore you with. The trials and tribulations of a somewhat grouchy older fellow are not the concern of anyone reading this. The remnants of a lost notebook or diary once belonging to one Doctor John H. Watson, however, are quite another matter.

It all began on a cold and quiet October morning. I had just opened the shop, and found there was only one customer patiently standing outside in the morning chill as I opened the door to let him in. Business of late had been admittedly slow — read *bad*, really bad. I was beginning to realize that in today's instant electronic computerized world, opening a so-called 'brick & mortar' bookstore might not have been the best business decision. However, I still loved books and my little store, and so did many other people. So I was happy to see at least one potential customer, and I welcomed this loner with quiet enthusiasm — though I noticed the small bag he carried under his arm with evident concern. I only hoped he was a buyer and not another seller. There were far too many of the latter these days, and never enough of the former.

'What can I do for you, my friend?' I said as he walked in and looked around, his young eyes scanning the shop, looking at all the various volumes surrounding us. He was a young man, tall and lean; but he seemed troubled, nervous. He made me a bit nervous as well. While he looked around, I went to the back counter and began to sip my morning coffee. Slowly he came closer to the counter and placed the bag down before me.

'I have something for you,' he told me softly. 'Would you like to buy it?'

I sighed. Another seller! Then I shrugged; I might as well see what it was that he had. Sometimes the most unusual and best items can come into a bookstore from a walk-in seller, so I said, 'Maybe. Depends on what it is.'

He nodded, like that seemed fair to him. Slowly he edged the mysterious bag closer and motioned for me to take a look. I was game, so I picked it up and looked inside the brown paper bag. Instantly my eyes lit up as I drew forth the contents. I'd not seen the likes of it in years.

'I know it's worth some good money,' the young man told me, and I could see an eager look enter his eyes that made him appear much more desperate than the average seller. He was rather young, but appeared to have fallen on hard times even at that youthful stage in his life, making his age seem greater than it actually was.

'I haven't seen one of these in many years,' I said truthfully, showing my awe, unable to hide it now. It was very nice, an almost pristine-condition copy of *The Strand Magazine* for July 1891. It was almost like new, with clean white pages and a bright sharp cover, and the issue in which was published the story *A Scandal in Bohemia*. That was the first Sherlock Holmes story to ever appear in *The*

Strand Magazine, and the one that set Holmes on the path to immortality. That is, after Holmes's first appearance in *Beeton's Christmas Annual* of 1887, of course, and *The Sign of The Four* in 1890. Then, in 1891, Doyle moved to London and set up a practice as an eye specialist — with not one single patient ringing his bell. So what to do? He began writing to pass the time — the doldrums, as Holmes might put it — and he wrote some new Sherlock Holmes short stories for the new *Strand Magazine*. Well, those tales caught fire, and the demand for more Holmes stories grew. Doyle supplied story after story, but only two years later he grew bored and irritated with Holmes and killed him off. Nevertheless, the name Sherlock Holmes would become known to every reader throughout the British Empire, and eventually the entire world.

What shocked me about this particular issue was that below the magazine title was a stamped inscription, the text of which proclaimed in large block letters 'AUTHOR COPY'. I was astounded, utterly surprised, but also growing skeptical by the moment.

What was this? Could it be real? I could barely realize my good fortune if it was. I looked it over carefully and determined that it was indeed authentic. Then I looked at the young man before me more closely and realized that he looked quite inauthentic. He didn't exactly look like a thief, but you could never tell these days. What did a thief look like, anyway?

'Where'd you get this?' I asked quickly, my fingers resisting the urge to pick up the magazine and begin leafing through it page by page. He didn't answer me. 'You stole it, didn't you?' I accused him boldly.

'You want it or not?' the kid asked sharply; then quickly scooped up the magazine, about to return it into the bag, when he suddenly stopped and looked me squarely in the eyes. 'For your information, it's not stolen. It's mine. It was handed down to me by my family. I inherited it. I just need to sell it.'

I didn't know what to say to that, but I knew I wanted that magazine. I had to have it! 'Okay, I'll take it,' I said, all thoughts of theft dropping from me like a shroud as I pulled out a crisp new fifty-dollar bill. The young man just laughed. I pulled out another fifty and set it down upon the counter in front of him beside the first bill. This time he merely smiled, and I grew nervous lest he leave the store with the priceless magazine, so I quickly doubled my offer again. Two more fifty-dollar bills joined the other two.

'Two hundred dollars,' I said sharply. I was nearing the limit of my cash reserves.

As if in deep thought, the young man seemed to weigh the situation impatiently, gave me a twisted leer, and then grabbed up the two hundred bucks and was soon gone from my shop. His seizing of the money had exposed his arm and the track marks that ran along it. They didn't look new, but I could tell he was a junkie. Who knew what part of his body he was using now to shoot up his poison? I immediately felt badly for the young man, because I had no doubt now what his next destination would be. I felt a twinge of sorrow for him, and guilt at my good fortune over his own misfortune. I admit it clouded my features as I examined the rare magazine he had left upon my counter. I had come upon an incredible item by a great stroke of luck, but the thought of how I had obtained it now only sickened me.

Well, was the magazine his, or was it stolen? Hot or not, the magazine was a gem and a classic, and it seemed to be the author's own copy. If it was . . . ? If it was, it would be priceless! But could what the young man said be true?

One of the reasons I had opened my bookstore in the first place was that books brought in for sale through the front door, while containing the usual dreck, often included some amazing finds. As a collector I often kept some of the more valuable items back home in my apartment, where I squirreled them away for reading, or later selling. But things like this did not happen every day. Things like this *do* happen sometimes in the book trade, though rarely. Was this one of those times? My heart skipped a beat as I thought about the possibilities.

I sat there alone in the quiet of my small shop, turning the hundred-year-old pages. I examined the magazine with the very greatest of care, and was surprised when I discovered a folded-up piece of paper that suddenly fell from inside the magazine onto the floor. Now what was this?

Immediately I picked up the slip of paper and examined it to see what it might be. It was a small sheet of quality paper, a page covered with small but intricate handwriting. Upon closer observation, I realized it was most certainly torn from some old book. Then I noticed the date of the entry — March 20, 1888. That was well over 120 years ago!

I stared at that date. It seemed to have some significance. Finally my old memory caught into gear, and from my readings I realized it was the probable date of the events Watson chronicled in the Sherlock Holmes story *A Scandal in Bohemia*. Was this a page from someone's notebook or diary? As I began to read the notes written there, I became even more astonished by what fate had put into my quivering hands. I now realized that it might be possible that what I held before me could be a page from the notebook of Doctor John H. Watson! Was it possible?

I now recalled a chapter from *The Hound of The Baskervilles*. The heading was entitled 'Extract From The Diary of Dr. Watson', so it was possible the good doctor kept an actual diary, and that it was not some literary device used by Doyle in his stories. I also remember from the stories that Watson often mentioned notebooks he kept full of information on Holmes's cases. So perhaps this was from one of those priceless notebooks? Notebook or diary, I knew the paper I held before me was a crucial page of incalculable value. But where was the rest of the book?

It was, indeed, an amazing find. I read it over and over, transfixed by what it might mean. By itself it might not at first appear all that earth-shattering — but the implications! The *implications*! On that one page I read where Watson had brilliantly outlined the case, placing particular emphasis on the interplay between Holmes and his female protagonist, Miss Irene Adler. In one note hastily scrawled within the margin was the sentence: 'Holmes seems to think the Irene Adler affair the best to recount now / rewrite from notes / then present draft / See what he thinks / JW 25/2/90.'

So there it was, all in the author's own hand — dated, and initialed; describing how on February 25th of 1890, John H. Watson, upon the recommendation of his friend Sherlock Holmes, decided to recount the facts of the Irene Adler affair into the fictionalized story *A Scandal in Bohemia*. Then he would send off the manuscript to his literary agent for submission and eventual publication, where it would appear in an issue of the prestigious *Strand Magazine* the next year, the July 1891 issue. The only thing that I could think of now was that this appeared to be proof that that story might not have been fiction at all! Which implied to me that some other things about Holmes and Watson might not be fiction as well. I was nearly hysterical with amazement and joy at the very thought. Dare I believe it?

Well, one thing I did know: I had a

priceless discovery in my hands. It was nothing less than a rare and valuable bit of historical evidence for the veracity of the Sherlock Holmes tales and perhaps even the very existence of Holmes and Watson themselves! Such a page was indeed priceless, and I held it delicately between my shaky old fingers, as reverently as any rare book dealer might hold an original copy of a Gutenberg Bible or the Dead Sea Scrolls. All the time the thought went spinning around in my mind like an arc of lightning — if this was just *one* page, then where was the rest of the notebook? Where was that sacred book now? Where was that book that held the greatest evidence of all time that Sherlock Holmes and Doctor Watson were *real* persons and not just works of fiction? I must find the rest of Watson's missing notebook!

I had to sit down, relax, and take a deep breath. I was totally flustered, wondering what to do next. I had stumbled upon something the likes of which I could never imagine. Then it came to me in a flash.

'The junkie!' I shouted out loud to the silent book-lined walls of my shop empty of all persons but myself. Quickly I gathered up the *Strand Magazine* and that priceless torn page and placed them securely into my safe. Then I closed the safe door and locked up the shop.

'I'm too old for this literary detective stuff,' I mumbled to myself as I quickly put on my coat and hat and left the store to feel the first cold blast of October air hit my bundled old body. Carefully, I scanned the area around my store and down the street in all directions, looking vainly for the young junkie; knowing that mine was most probably a hopeless quest. Nevertheless, I began to walk and walk and walk down the street, passing one block and then the next, going out of one neighborhood and into another one much less savory. I went where my feet and my heart told me to go.

I'd last seen the kid walking east on Rutherford, probably to make a drug score, so I continued my trek on down that cold and windy block. I passed all the sterile and lonely apartment buildings and all the cold and lonely neighborhood people until I came to a certain corner. I was far away from the safe part of town where my store was located, with all those cute trendy shops, where there were police, good citizens, and always law and order. And safety. Not so out here. This was the hinterlands.

I now found myself in a different world. You know about corners like these — most old or poor neighborhoods have them; the corners where the local hoods hang out and where the junkies go to get their fixes. I noticed four young men in a small group hanging out in front of one of the worst-looking houses I'd ever seen. It was decrepit, neglected, run-down, most assuredly a drug den. They stood out front warming their hands over a fire raging in a garbage can, passing around a bottle and laughing about something. Were they junkies on the prowl? Guards set to alert the dealers to the cops? Pushers? Or just harmless neighborhood kids? I couldn't tell, but I knew I'd find out soon enough. I knew this was dangerous, even stupid, but I could not go back now. I had to find that kid; had to ask him . . . questions . . . find out . . . find out exactly what?

I took a deep breath and walked over to the four young men by the blazing fire, my old bones rattling with fear and the cold, vaguely wondering if one of these four had been the one who had mugged me last month — wondering if they were actually planning it again now. They continued to talk and laugh and pass around a bottle that was surely some kind of alcohol, but they watched me sharply while I approached them.

An old man. An easy target. What was I getting myself into?

'*Viejo, gringo*,' one said loudly, rather defiantly. Then he looked at me closely and just laughed, offering me a hit on his bottle. Suddenly I realized that I knew the kid. He was John — or Juan, actually, and he'd come into my store one day a long time ago to look around at all the books. It had been years ago, when I'd first opened my store and used to sell old collector's books before they became just too expensive. I remembered that one of those old Sherlock Holmes books had caught Juan's fancy. I think it was a mint facsimile copy of the Holmes stories as they had originally appeared in *The Strand Magazine*, with those wonderful Sidney Paget illustrations. It was a nice book, not particularly valuable, but out of print in that edition. Years before, you could actually find them fairly easily; but by then, like a lot of books, certain editions seemed to have become scarce.

Well, Juan really liked that book, but no way did he have the money to buy it. I was concerned he might try to steal it, or even rob my store, but then I realized I was just being paranoid and began to feel a bit guilty. The kid simply loved the book; it was plain to see he was fascinated by it. He just had no money to buy it. It was then that some might say a form of bookish generosity, or bookseller insanity, must have overcome me, and I decided to just give him the book. It was a gift. I do that sometimes. Bookselling is about getting the right book into the hands of the right person. Money, while always nice, and certainly necessary to continue in business, should never be the sole determining factor in placing the right book in the hands of the right person who would cherish it. It has never been with me. That book was a gift. When I told him it was his, he could not believe it. The smile of sheer joy on his face was price enough in return for me. He left my store with a wildly shouted *Gracias!* He had never come back since. But I saw him from time to time in the neighborhood around the stores, and he always had a cheery *Gracias* and a big smile for me. That had been enough.

Well, now Juan was a lot older and a lot tougher-looking — and I was an old man feeling like he was about to get blown over any moment if the cold wind grew any stronger. Juan held out the bottle; I nodded my thanks and took a short swallow. I didn't usually drink, and certainly not like this, but now it seemed the thing to do. I did not want to insult these kids. It was cheap wine, as I had expected, but it warmed my insides, and for that I was grateful.

'*Gracias*, Juan,' I said and passed him

back the bottle. The other three guys watched me and laughed a bit making fun of the old man. *Gringo, Viejo*, they called me, and laughed. But it was not mean, dangerous laughter — they smiled and nodded good-naturedly; so I decided to continue with my mission.

'I'm looking for a kid, Juan. Can you help me please?' I told him, trying to get some warmth from the blazing fire into my numb fingers.

Juan shrugged and looked at his boys. They shrugged back without any answer.

'He came into my store and sold me something. You know I have the bookstore on Dorchester? Well, I gave him some money, but when he left I could see the marks on his arm. I knew he'd be coming down here to score. I need to talk to him. Is he inside?'

'Are you crazy? You want to go inside that house?' Juan said, showing concern I'd never expected. 'Go home — go back to your little store and all your books. This is a bad place for you, *Viejo*.'

'You know that kid, Juan? A tall Anglo with blond hair, wearing a black coat and old jeans? Is he inside now?'

'He's inside, but by now he's gone into dreamland.'

'I have to talk to him!' I insisted. 'Can I go inside? Or could you bring him out to talk to me?'

'They'll take you apart in there, old man,' Juan said nervously.

'Hey, man!' one of Juan's boys shouted. 'What you want here?'

'Yeah, go home old man, before you get hurt!' another barked in warning.

'Go home, *Viejo*,' Juan said more kindly, patting my shoulder. 'The kid's name is Joe. I'll tell him to come to your store, all right — but *manana* — *ahora* you must go! *Vaya!*'

So I went. I took the long walk in the searing cold back home to my apartment, which was located a few blocks down the street from my store. All the time my mind reeled at the thought of the existence of that diary or notebook, and what exactly a sick little junkie named Joe knew about it all.

2

A Most Unlikely Team-Up

The next day was a long and quiet one in my store. Only a few customers came in, mostly housewives who bought the latest James Patterson or John Sandford thrillers — sales for which I was grateful — but there was no Joe. It was almost closing time when the bell over the door announced that I had another visitor. Another customer? It might just be a red-letter day for customers in my small bookshop. I looked up to see that it was Juan.

'Hey, *Viejo*,' he said with his easy smile, slowly walking toward the counter in the back. I was ensconced there like a king on his throne and the kid approached me with an easy, confident stride. I watched him approach, young and bold. Like most young people, he could have the world in his pocket at that age, if only he was smart enough — and lucky. I was a different matter; at my age, the world had me right where it wanted me — old and under its thumb. So great to be young, I thought. I remember being that once. A wonderful — and terrible — time. I watched carefully as the young man's sharp, bright eyes scanned all the shelves filled with books all around him in awe. I could tell he liked books, but they also seemed to intimidate him.

'Hello, Juan. Thanks for coming by. Did you see Joe?'

Juan smiled easily and changed the subject. 'You know, you have a nice store here. All these old books are real nice. I used to like books, but that was before I dropped out of school — and boy, was that a bad move! But that's the way the game is played in my part of town. I remember when you let me have that book, old man. You know, I sold it for a hundred bucks!'

'I didn't know that. Did you read it first, at least?' I asked, feeling vaguely hurt that my moment of generosity had resulted in such mercenary behavior. You don't sell gifts.

'Yeah, I did read it, every word — and it was great, man! Like, I still remember when Holmes fought Moriarty, and all those adventures with his best friend Doctor Watson. They were great! The London fog, the hansom cabs, everything. It was a different world back then, for sure. Maybe a better world?'

Not a better world, but I didn't want to dissuade Juan's enthusiasm just then. I had another thought on my mind. I couldn't resist asking him, with a hint of sarcasm in my voice, 'So you got a hundred bucks for the book? I seem to remember I was selling it for only twenty. Maybe you should be in the book business, Juan?'

'Yeah, sometimes I think it would be nice — crazy and stupid to do these days — but maybe nice. Yeah, I got a hundred from some *gringo*, I mean Anglo, collector in my school. He thought I stole it but didn't ask me no questions. I let him think so — I think he liked the idea that it might have been hot — like I was some great cat burglar or something. Some Latino Raffles.'

'A hundred bucks is a lot for a kid. What did you do with the money?' I asked carefully, trying not to let suspicion enter my voice. 'I guess you bought yourself music CDs or clothes?'

'Hey, man, don't play that stuff with me when you really wanna ask me if I bought drugs! Right?'

I was stunned by his candor for a moment, and then realized he was right. I did want to ask him that, and I feared what his answer might be. Now I had to ask myself if my gift to him years ago had allowed him to get money to buy drugs. Had it been the cause of his downfall, instead of something I thought would help him? I sighed and hoped desperately that it was not, then I said, 'I'm sorry, but I need to know. Did you buy drugs with the money?'

Juan laughed lightly. 'Shit no! Dope is for dopes, *Viejo*. I never touched that stuff until a year ago, and now I'm off it altogether. When I was a kid back then — when you knew me — I was clean, man. I used the bread to buy my family Christmas presents. It was the best

Christmas I ever gave them — and the last one we all shared together. Things got really bad after that. I don't like to talk about it.'

Well, I couldn't say too much about that. I knew Juan did not want to go into details of his private personal history — and I didn't want to press him — but I was glad to hear that the small gift of that book so long ago had had some good effects.

'So what about Joe? Where is he?' I asked, changing the subject.

Juan shrugged and then looked at me straight in the eyes, hard, saying coldly, 'I went to talk to him, *Viejo*, but by the time I found him he was dead. OD — heroin.'

'Oh my God!' I hardly knew what to say, or how to react; I was so surprised, so sad. I mumbled something like, 'That's too bad.'

'That's what the pushers say too,' Juan replied acidly. 'You know, they hate to lose a good customer that way, but there's plenty more buyers around, plenty more where he came from. Pushers don't starve.'

'That's what everyone says when they are powerless to prevent something bad from happening, or they don't know what to do about something, or just don't give a damn. It's the pushers who don't give a damn. I understand them, or at least the mentality, but I'm not like them. See, I'm a pusher too, in my own way, Juan. I'm a pusher of books. Though a book never killed anyone, and it's probably the only addiction that's actually good for you.'

'You're a smart old man — you know a lot of weird stuff from those books, I think — but I think you read too much. Get into the real world, *Viejo*! Open your eyes. So what did you want to talk to Joe about, anyway?'

'He sold me something,' I said carefully, 'and I wanted to ask him where he got it.'

'A book?'

'An old magazine. Did you ever hear of *The Strand Magazine*?'

'*Viejo, Viejo*, I'm poor and Latino, not *estúpido*. Do you know that since you turned me on to books, I've read all the Sherlock Holmes stories? Every damn one! All fifty-six short stories, plus the four novels. Sometimes I even read a short one before I go to sleep at night — you know, to get, like, just a taste — *The Red-Headed League* or *Silver Blaze* . . . or . . . '

'*A Scandal in Bohemia*?'

'Yeah, now that was one fine-ass story! I liked that girl . . . '

'Irene Adler.'

'Yeah, Irene Adler. She had real guts. Smart, too!'

I smiled. 'Holmes liked her as well.' I had made my decision: I would trust this young man. I walked over, opened my safe, and took out the copy of the *Strand* and the torn page from what I considered might just be Watson's notebook. I placed them on the countertop in front of Juan and then walked over to the door and locked it, putting up the CLOSED sign. Then I came back to Juan at the counter.

He was carefully looking over the magazine and the torn page. He had not picked them up yet, fearful to even touch, but I could see he was examining them intently. Mere curiosity hardly described his fascination. He looked them over for quite a while, silently. I did likewise, still amazed by what had come into my possession. Finally, I heard him mutter a few words in quick Spanish that my old ears could not catch; then he looked up at me suspiciously and asked, 'What is this?'

'What do you think it is? You said you've read Sherlock Holmes,' I replied acidly.

'Yeah, but . . . This is old . . . and it looks real! That can't be possible! Is that possible?'

'I think so, Juan. I really think so,' I said, my voice showing the awe that I felt overwhelming me.

'*Sheet!*'

'Yes, *sheet* indeed.'

'And you bought it from Joe? Where the hell would he get something like this, *Viejo*?'

'I have no idea. He said it was in his family. That's what I want you to help me find out, Juan.'

'Me? Oh, really?'

'I'm not a young man, Juan. At sixty-two, I have a lot of mileage on this broken-down old body. You're young, strong, you have energy, and you know people — not the sort of people I know, and that can be helpful. What it boils down to is that I need your help. Maybe we could find the rest of the book — that diary or notebook or whatever it is that was written by Watson himself — a historical document that might prove the existence of Sherlock Holmes. Think of it! What do you say?'

He looked at me like I was insane, and sputtered, 'I don't know. It sounds *loco*.'

'Crazy? Yeah, I guess. But think of it, Juan — *we* could do it! Together! It would be the greatest discovery since Stanley found Livingstone!'

'Since who found who? You're a crazy *viejo*.' Juan laughed dismissively, then he looked over the torn page once more, and finally just smiled. 'But I guess I'm just as damn crazy as you are. Where do we begin?'

3

A Watson/Holmes Connection?

We began the next morning by tracking down Joe's family. We found them in a little semi-detached wood-frame house near the Heights. They didn't know much. Joe's mother had passed away years before. His father seemed to have disappeared right after Joe's birth — run off, most likely — and he was never seen again. The grandparents raised Joe — or Joseph, as they preferred to call him — and they seemed to know little about his life other than superficial information. He was an only child. They were an aged couple not in the best of health, and they seemed to live mostly in the past. I guess I couldn't blame them.

We introduced ourselves. Juan told them, 'I am Juan Marcano, and this is my companion, Professor Thomas Jones; he's retired from the local college.'

They nodded, smiled wanly, then introduced themselves as Herman and Amelia Adler. At the mention of that name, Juan and I looked at each other with obvious surprise, but did not say a word yet.

We all shook hands. They seemed to be nice people; friendly, but happy to be secluded in their own small world. It was a world even more detached than my own. Juan looked at them, then back at me, and just shook his head. Then he winked at me. Finally, he couldn't hold it in any longer, and whispered, 'Adler?' He said the name as if it were some magical word — which, for us, it surely was.

I nodded. I had recognized the name, of course; but even more so, I could feel there was something here mysterious and uncovered. I said to the elderly couple, 'I'm sorry about the loss of your grandson.'

They nodded. Herman told us, 'Thank you, but I'm not surprised to tell you that we expected something like this from Joseph . . . someday. He was a wild youth, and much too independent for us to control.'

'Well, we are very sorry,' I repeated, not knowing what else to say.

'Are you with the police?' Mrs. Adler inquired.

'No,' I told her carefully, hoping that would not mess up my plans, 'but we're trying to discover some information that your Joseph might have known.'

'Did you know Joseph?' she asked softly, her eyes welling with tears.

'No,' I answered slowly, not wanting to mess this up. 'I did meet him once a few days ago, when he sold me an old magazine. I needed to ask him about that. It is rather important.'

'I see,' she said softly, nodding.

I sat down next to the old lady, carefully considerate, smiling, and told her about Joseph selling me the old magazine. 'Mrs. Adler, could you tell us where your grandson might have found a copy of *The Strand Magazine* from 1891? It is British, and not a common item here — rather rare, actually.'

She shrugged. It didn't seem to mean anything to her. I began to see that she was just a bit off. A touch of senility, perhaps? Or she had just given up on life after so many long, hard years, with so much bitter disappointment?

Her husband Herman, obviously in his late eighties, seemed to think hard for a minute, then added, 'You know, Amelia, I bet you Joseph took that magazine from my father's old papers up in the attic.'

Mrs. Adler's eyes lit up and she nodded, as if that could be true.

I looked over at Juan; he gave me a slight grin, the light of discovery in his own big brown eyes. 'And Mr. Adler, I have to ask you something, if you don't mind?'

'Yes?' he replied curiously.

'Did you ever hear of the actress Irene Adler?'

'Oh, her — why yes, of course. That would be my grandmother Irene, back just after the turn of the century. So long ago. My father, Jack, he was her son. Never spoke of her much; I don't think they got along. Granny was a bit of a . . . well, she was a wild woman even for them times. They called her an adventuress . . . but that wasn't really a very nice thing to be known as back then.'

'I see,' I replied softly, fighting to restrain my enthusiasm from bursting into a wild shout of awe and victory. I looked to Juan and saw him staring in open-mouthed surprise. I told him to close his mouth. He did, then smiled like the cat who'd swallowed the canary.

Mr. Adler continued in a faraway voice, remembering. 'Of course, Jack passed on the Adler name to me, and I passed that name to my son, Joseph. My grandson's father was Joseph senior, but he left right after the boy was born. Bastard! I assume that is one reason why Joseph has always been a troublesome only child, so wild — much like his great-grandmother, I imagine. That wildness and lack of discipline, linked with the use of drugs, proved a deadly combination for our poor grandson. He couldn't handle it in the end, I guess. I don't see how anyone can, really. Drugs finally took his life. It was not a surprise to us. Anyway, it seems to be the end of the Adler family name.'

It was sad, tragic. We were quiet for a long moment. The old man and woman trying to stifle their tears. It was obvious they dearly loved their grandson, but had not understood him at all; the age difference was just too great between them, and there was little real communication or comprehension.

Herman Adler looked at his wife with determination and nodded. I wondered what that might mean, then I found out.

'There's an old tin box upstairs, Professor Jones,' the wife suddenly told me, looking back at her husband for confirmation. 'Herman, why not take them up there and show it to them?'

I looked at Juan, barely able to restrain my enthusiasm, but neither of us said a word. We knew to keep mum for now.

Mr. Adler slowly walked Juan and me across the room to the stairs, up to the second floor, then up another row of stairs into a dusty cobweb-filled attic. There was no light fixture, so we walked across the creaking floorboards with flashlight in hand, the beam focused on a pile of old Victorian furniture and hangings in the far corner. Herman slowly walked us towards that wall. He shined his light on a small empty rectangular spot that was bordered by recently disturbed dust.

'That's strange. I don't understand it, gentlemen. That little tin box was always right there. It was here the last time I looked. Now it's gone. I don't know how that could happen; no one ever comes up here, not even Amelia and I. Maybe Joseph, I imagine. But I can't fathom what Joseph junior could have wanted with old Grandpa Adler's things and all. Just a pile of old junk, if you ask me.'

I nodded, but I was totally crushed that my dreams of seeing that old tin box, and what it might hold, were now gone. Par for the course, I thought.

Herman trained his flashlight beam on all four walls of the attic in a vain attempt to seek out the location of the old tin box. He murmured, 'Maybe Joseph moved it?'

I nodded. It seemed like a logical explanation. At least, I hoped it would prove true, and I prayed that we might find it soon. But it was all in vain; the tin box was obviously not there. If it had in fact ever been there, it was gone now.

I thanked the elderly couple for their time, and we took our leave. As we got outside, Juan turned to me. 'Prof, this is much more involved than anything I ever imagined. It's just like Sherlock Holmes himself would say: when you take away the impossible, whatever remains is the probable.'

'Well, Juan,' I offered thoughtfully, 'that's not exactly a perfect quote, but I get your drift.'

'No you don't, Prof. You been selling books too long and not reading them. This here is a Sherlock Holmes case. The old tin box is missing. I'll tell you something else: this Joseph Adler did not OD. He was murdered, maybe to keep him quiet about what he'd discovered in that old tin box.'

'Murdered?' I asked, surprised by his statement and the seemingly absolute certainty of it.

'Yes, *Viejo*, no doubt. And it has to do with what is in that old tin box,' Juan told me, but he would not go into detail when I prompted him further. I waited for some evidence. That would have been nice.

'But how do you know this?' I finally asked him again.

'Elementary, that's what it is.'

I shook my head dubiously.

'No, really, *Viejo*, that's what it is — elementary. I'll tell you what else: I read about Watson's old banged-up travel box in the stories — this might be it!'

'So you think this box might be Watson's travel-worn and battered tin dispatch box?' I asked curiously, hope straining with disbelief and incredulity within me and ready to burst forth. But I restrained myself and quietly said, 'Very interesting.'

'Yes, I imagine it very well could be.'

'The box that the Holmes stories told of, resided somewhere in the vaults of the bank Cox & Co., at Charing Cross in London, England. If this is it, whatever is it doing here in America — and in Dorchester, of all places?'

'What indeed?' Juan replied with an enigmatic smile.

4

Bookstore Shakedown

Juan and I were back at my bookshop. I locked the door. There wasn't any threat of a horde of customers disturbing us, but I wanted to be careful and not have us disturbed. I wanted privacy while we talked things out. We had a lot to discuss.

'So this Joseph Junior was the great-grandson of Irene Adler,' I stated thoughtfully, in an effort to put into order what we knew, or thought he knew, fervently trying to hold back the enthusiasm I felt. Of course, at that point it was all just theory, conjecture, assumptions, and just plain hope; but stranger things have happened. 'It's truly amazing if it is true, but it seems impossible.'

'Irene Adler . . . *and* Sherlock Holmes? They made a baby!' Juan added, allowing his astonishment to show through the brightness of his face, his eyes wide, a broad grin of triumph. 'That would make Joseph Adler Sherlock Holmes's great-great grandson.'

I nodded, but then I could see something was bothering Juan about all this. 'What is it?'

'But why Adler? Why not Holmes for the last name of their son?' he asked me curiously.

'Ah, yes,' I said thoughtfully. That was the question, but there had to be a reason for that. 'Well, perhaps she kept her own name? Not a common occurrence back then, for sure, but Irene Adler was a famous stage actress. Women in that line of work usually kept their last names, even when they married. Even back then. For all we know, Adler might not have been her real name.'

Juan just nodded. 'There's something else. If the child was Holmes's son, he would have wanted to protect the boy. He could have done that by giving him the Adler last name, and not the Holmes last name. The Holmes last name would have made the child a target of Holmes's enemies. Whatever the reason, we know *something* was done back then, because the Adler name continued with Joseph to the present day.'

I shook my head in consternation. This was all a bit too much for me, and I felt that Juan was getting far ahead of himself on this. However, I was hard pressed to deflate his youthful enthusiasm, even though I knew we needed to be careful. 'We don't know that for sure. Indeed, it was mentioned that Irene Adler married another man after her encounter with Holmes in *Scandal*, if you remember what took place in the Doyle story, but I think she became a widow years later. Her life is certainly a foggy mystery. We don't even know if she and Holmes ever met again, much less had a real affair . . . '

'You mean, had sex?'

'Yes — crudely put, but essentially correct. They would have had to do that in order for Irene to become pregnant with Holmes's baby.'

'No shit, Sherlock!' Juan blurted with an unrestrained laugh. I could see my young friend was having a bit of fun at my expense.

'Very funny, young man. I guess you just couldn't resist saying that, but can you get serious for a minute, please?'

'Yes, I am always serious . . . but Irene Adler could have had an affair later on with Holmes. Who knows if they hooked up later, Prof? Could be.'

'I imagine anything is possible,' I sighed, confused and overwhelmed by it all. Was it actually possible? My mind was reeling.

'Yeah,' Juan added sharply, 'Irene and Holmes did know each other, so there was that connection for sure. It's stated in the Holmes story. And I think they even loved each other. Again surmised in the Holmes story. However, I think the significant thing now for us is that Joseph Adler didn't OD, he was murdered.'

'Why do you keep saying that? How can you be so sure? That would be hard to prove in any case,' I offered, somewhat annoyed. He was stating something that he had no proof of; but the more I thought about it, I had to admit I had the same feeling churning in my gut. We had no evidence, but I also felt something was very wrong with this young man's death.

'Simple enough, *Viejo*. We find out. Can't you get a copy of the doctor's report? You know, when they do the autopsy?'

I looked at my young companion and nodded at his bright idea. 'You know, Juan, I still have some academic contacts. I might just be able to arrange that. Pull some strings, eh? I'll put it on the list of things to do tomorrow. Meanwhile, what do we do now?'

Juan thought about my question for a moment, and then said, 'I've been thinking about just that. I want us to investigate this case like Holmes and Watson would have done. I've read all the books, and so have you, and even if I can't quote the stories line by line, I know the meaning — the feel of them . . . ' He hesitated, as if almost fearful to continue, then he looked me in the eyes directly and added softly, 'You know, those stories are like poetry to me, and I feel that poetry inside me, *Viejo*. Do you want to partner with me, and we'll work this murder case together?'

I smiled. It was tempting, and a nice gesture from this young man to include me in what I considered to be his rather fantastic insane delusion. However, I still had a bookstore to run. I had internet book orders to process, new books to unpack and shelve, a flyer to put together for a special author signing coming up, and . . .

And yet, isn't it true that there is always something in the way of us doing the things we want to do? Isn't there? Or the things we know we *should* do. I sighed, seeing the fire that burned in Juan's youthful eyes, and I had to admit I felt that same fire burning within me also. It was the lure of adventure. The game was afoot! We *could* find out the truth. *Had* Joseph Adler really been murdered? *What* was in that battered tin box? Were the two events connected? There were many questions that came to me, and each one of them cried out for an answer.

I said, 'Juan, I'm an old man. I don't know what to do about this. I'm afraid I can't fight or even help you very much if things get, you know, rough.'

'*Viejo*, that's all right. Holmes wanted Watson with him because of his good advice, his common sense, his wisdom.'

'I'm afraid I have very little of that to offer you.'

'More than I, *Viejo*.'

I gave him a lopsided grin of utter surprise, suddenly wondering just what was going on here. 'Wait one minute! Let me get this straight. Am I mistaken, or are you automatically placing *me* in the role of Watson? Thereby humbly placing *yourself*, I suspect, in the role of the great Sherlock Holmes?'

Juan only shrugged as if it was the most natural thing in the world and gave me a sly grin. 'I tell you, *jefe*, I have these stories in my soul. Joseph Adler was murdered to shut him up about what was in that tin box. That missing box has material in it over a hundred and twenty years old. What could it possibly contain that could be a threat to anyone today? What could it contain that anyone would kill for?'

'Indeed, Holmes,' I chided with a repressed smile, in what I thought was my best Watson-type voice. I would accept my Watson role if I had to for the moment, but refused to be compared to the sweet but bumbling Nigel Bruce version. 'This seems to be a case that contains some hitherto unknown considerations.'

'That is true,' Juan stated simply.

'You know, it may not be murder at all,' I added. 'I think you are taking a big leap here in your theory.'

Juan nodded with a thoughtful grin. 'Perhaps — but see, I am already correct: you do make a fine Watson.'

I shook my head and shrugged, accepting my role for the time being, but not appreciating it at all. In fact, I was rather rankled by it. Really, how could he — this young pup of a wise-ass kid, dare put himself in the footsteps of the great Sherlock Holmes? I was the older of us. I was much more knowledgeable, experienced, worldly — I had it all. So if anyone should play the role of Holmes in this situation, it should be me!

I looked at Juan, a young tough kid. Then I realized just how silly and petty I was being about it all and felt rather ashamed of myself. I sighed with defeat, deciding to go along with Juan's fantasy detective role-playing game for the time being if it made him happy.

'Besides,' Juan continued, interrupting my thoughts, 'Watson fulfills another valuable role for Holmes.'

'Okay, I'll bite. What could that be?'

Juan smiled, carefully went into his pocket, and pulled out a nickel-plated snub-nosed .38, and handed it to me saying, 'Watson is the one who has to hold the revolver.'

I looked askance at Juan as he placed the weapon in my hands, then stared at the object with utter disdain. 'Oh no, not a gun!' I held it out to him, but he would not take it back.

'Just in case we need it, *Viejo*. No one would search or suspect an old man like you; and remember, we're investigating a murder case now. Things could become dangerous.'

'I don't like it, Juan.'

'Hold on to it. We may need it before this case is over.'

'Where did you get this?'

'Don't worry about that now.'

Reluctantly I had to admit he might be right, so I slipped the .38 into my pocket. That was one second before I heard the loud crash of breaking glass at one of the front windows of my store. Instantly all was utter chaos, and then something suddenly fell with a thump to my feet.

'What the hell!' I blurted in alarm. 'What's this?'

Juan looked at the thing. It appeared to be a paving stone from the cobbled street outside my store, or perhaps a small package. But he reacted instantly, shoving me down behind the counter with him. We hunkered down, nervous, waiting.

'What? Do you think it's a bomb?' I whispered, astonished — and terrified now.

Nothing happened. No explosion. The only sound was my harsh breathing.

'It's not a bomb,' Juan laughed, telling me with evident relief, as if he might have been expecting just such a thing. I shuddered, sighing deeply with fear. I looked at the broken window of my store. All that glass all over the place. What a mess!

Juan picked up the thing to show me and I could see now that it was indeed a brick. 'It has a message on it, *Viejo*. There are words written upon it. See? As Holmes would say, a rather crude but effective way of gaining our attention.'

'Yeah, crude but effective, my ass!'

Juan just laughed, examining the brick closely like he was looking for clues.

'What does it say, Juan?' I asked impatiently, coming out from behind the counter, eyeing the damage to the right front window of my store. It was a mess. I would have to get the glass replaced tomorrow. For now I'd have to board up the window with a sheet of plywood before I left the store to go home tonight. I was annoyed. This just meant more work, more expense. But it was really frightening to have this kind of thing happening to me, and to my store. Nothing like this ever happened in this part of town.

'Ah, see this here, just two words on the brick: 'STOP' and 'DEATH',' Juan stated simply with a smile, and damn if the kid didn't look excited by what had happened.

'How melodramatic,' I muttered, really angry now, but also finding that I was shaking. Was it fear? Anger? More like sheer terror, I realized. I tried to calm down. What did it mean?

'How to the point. Simple, yet a very effective message,' Juan told me, obviously channeling his inner Sherlock as he carefully examined the brick again. 'And certainly attention-grabbing. I am afraid there is nothing I can glean from this other than the message itself, and the fact that someone is very serious about us not looking into the Joseph Adler murder. We have an enemy, *Viejo*, one who has yet to show himself, but it is someone who is quite serious about us not pursuing the Adler murder. For now, we have been given a warning, next time . . . '

'Juan, we don't even know if Adler was murdered at all,' I stated simply.

'Oh, I think this little message tells us that now quite clearly.'

I just looked at him intently, afraid now that he might be right. Later on I got out a piece of plywood from the back room and Juan helped me board up the broken window. Then we went home for the night. We each had a lot on our minds.

5

What the Autopsy Told Us

The next morning I never made it to my bookstore at all. No sooner did I get out of bed, wash and get dressed than I heard a constant ringing at my downstairs doorbell. When I answered it I discovered that it was Juan Marcano all bright-eyed and bushy-tailed and set to get to work on our case.

'Do you have any idea what time it is, Juan?' I asked, quite exasperated at being disturbed at that time of the morning. I was not a morning person. I mean, it was not even 7 a.m. yet! I hadn't even had my first cup of coffee, and I'm no good at all without that first cup of morning coffee.

'I hear you old folks go to sleep early and rise early so I knew you'd be ready to get started as soon as possible this morning,' Juan told me simply, but all I saw was the arrogance of youth in his statement and it irked me. I glared at him as I got myself together. Old? I'd show him! He was in my small living room, watching me tuck in my shirt and put on my tie.

'You have a lot of books here, you know that, *Viejo*?' he said with a crooked smile as he looked around my apartment at the shelves crammed with my collection. He was right; my tiny apartment was crammed with shelves of old, rare books.

I just grunted, angered. That age remark still rankled.

'*Andale, Viejo!*' Juan chided me rapidly, full of impatience.

'You always barge in on people so early?' I barked back in annoyance.

'No, *Viejo*, never; but you are a special case. I need you. We have to take a ride downtown to see your friend, Doctor Williams, at the city morgue, to get a look at that autopsy report for Joseph Adler.'

I sighed. The kid was proving a harsh taskmaster. 'I'm sorry I ever mentioned him to you last night, Juan. I'm sure you're setting yourself up for a major disappointment. Adler wasn't murdered;

he was a drug addict and he OD'ed. That's it, and it is that simple. Sad, but simple.'

'And what about that brick thrown through your store window last night? That was no accident,' Juan reminded me.

I had almost forgotten that. I think I had wanted to forget it. I looked up at him sharply, annoyed. I *had* forgotten about that! Those two cryptic words, 'STOP' and 'DEATH', meant it was more than common vandalism. The message wasn't all that cryptic, and it certainly didn't take a Sherlock Holmes to realize that it was not good.

I sighed deeply, resigned to my fate. It seemed we were slowly sinking into what could become a dangerous mess, and I was afraid it was going to get deeper before it got better. If it got better. I tied my tie and put on my blazer, then finished my coffee.

'Don't forget your revolver,' Juan reminded me quickly, pointing to where I'd left it on the living room coffee table.

'You really think . . . ?'

'Yes, *Viejo*, I do. Remember the brick and the note last night, and don't forget that Adler was murdered.'

'*Maybe* Adler was murdered, but I still think he probably OD'ed,' I replied firmly. At least it would have made things a lot simpler for me had that been the case. But if he *was* murdered . . . ? Then we . . . I owed that boy a chance for justice. I sighed deeply. Nothing important is ever simple.

'Maybe he OD'ed on heroin, but he was most *certainly* murdered, *Viejo*. I tell you this is true,' Juan insisted forcefully.

'You can be a rather bull-headed young man, you know that, Juan?'

Juan just smiled back at me. 'Yes, much like Mr. Holmes, I imagine.'

'Hah!' I blurted.

He just smiled and pointed to the revolver.

I nodded, picked up the small snub-nosed .38 and slipped it into my blazer pocket, where I was relieved to see that it showed hardly any lines at all.

'All right, Holmes,' I chided my young pest, 'lead the way.'

* * *

The Dorchester city morgue was a cold, stark place. Cold because the bodies in it had to be kept 'fresh' as they were being worked on, so there was a constant chill in the air. The place was stark with the white, empty bleakness and antiseptic odor of a large hospital operating room. Or a meat packing plant.

My friend and colleague from the old days, Doctor Theodore 'Ted' Williams, whom I had called the night before, met us at the loading dock where I had parked my old Chevy Aveo. It was in Williams's reserved parking spot out back, where he had told me to park.

'Good to see you, Tommy, old man,' Ted told me cordially with a smile and a kindly slap upon the back.

'You know, Ted, this youngster here, Juan, keeps calling me *Viejo* — old man — and now you're doing it. It's not what I want to hear these days,' I told him with a hint of sarcasm through my good humor. 'After all, I'm retired, not dead. Not yet.'

'*Jefe* has many more good years to go,' Juan pointed out with a knowing grin.

I looked at him sternly and muttered, 'Yeah, thanks.' I shook my head in exasperation at Juan, then my attention focused back to Dr. Williams. 'So, Ted, I'm glad you could meet us on such short notice.'

'No problem. I take it what you are doing is unofficial?'

I nodded carefully. 'Yes, quite unofficial. Do you mind?'

Dr. Williams grinned. 'Well, it's not a problem for me, you know. I'm glad to do it for old time's sake, Tommy. I have what you wanted. Here it is. A copy of the autopsy report for one Joseph Adler. Not my work, though. It was performed by a different doctor.'

He handed me the copy and I thumbed through it carefully. It was several pages long, including diagrams and various other reports appended. I looked for the key item I was interested in, the toxicology report, but I did not see it.

'What does it say, Doc?' Juan asked Doctor Williams impatiently. 'Can you give us the bottom line?'

Williams nodded. 'The toxicology isn't back yet from the lab — it'll take another day or three — but I can tell you this now. The autopsy says your friend died from a drug overdose, but I am sure he was definitely murdered. Whether he was on drugs or not at the time of his death, there are indications of blunt force trauma on the back of his head that don't lie. I don't know why this was disregarded in the report.'

'Why is his death listed here in the police report as an accident?' I asked, wondering at the determination made by the policemen on the scene who had found Adler's body. The cops seemed to agree with the autopsy, but Williams didn't. Why?

Williams shrugged. 'The cops on the scene reported that the death was the result of a drug OD, and that in the course of overdosing the man then fell down and apparently cracked his head in the fall, and that's what they say killed him.'

I shook my head in alarm. This didn't seem right at all. 'I don't know.'

Juan just muttered, 'A pipe to the head or a baseball bat, more than likely.'

I nodded, looked intently at Williams. 'You signed off on this, Ted?'

'No, absolutely not,' Dr. Williams replied with a hint of sarcasm. 'Look, the cops just want to clear the caseload. A junkie dies, they call it an accident and it gets taken off their books. That's all they care about, closing cases. I'm waiting for the toxicology to get back, because while I'm certain that the boy was high on something when he died, drugs didn't kill him. However, neither did any fall, even though the cops have listed that in their interpretation of events. However, I'm just looking at the report as a favor to you. I didn't do the autopsy, so that leaves some items open.'

'Did you have a chance to examine the body before . . . you know?' Juan asked Williams.

'Yes, that's why I feel the way I do about the death.'

Juan looked at me, confused. I could feel his hot temper was growing, so I knew I had to kick in with something right away. But nothing too accusatory. 'I don't understand,' I said, looking squarely at Williams now, my surprise obvious.

'Joseph Adler had drugs in his system that probably killed him,' Doctor Williams explained, 'but he was also hit on the head. Not badly enough to kill him, I believe, but surely seriously enough to cause unconsciousness. I believe he may have been *given* the drugs then, involuntarily. Of course the toxicology may give us a clue about that. If Adler had more drugs in his system than he would be able to give himself in one dose — an unusually large amount, for example — then it could mean foul play.'

'Adler was knocked out, then given a hot shot, *Viejo*,' Juan explained with a knowing nod of his head. Then my young friend looked at me and the doctor. Williams remained silent and did not dispute his words.

'So he *was* murdered!' I blurted, alarmed now by the truth.

'I believe so,' Williams told us. 'And once I see the final reports, I'll bring this up with the medical board and the police.'

I nodded. That was good enough for me. 'So it was probable murder. I can't believe it.' I looked over at Juan and sighed deeply, 'You were right.'

'I told you so, *Viejo*,' was all the kid said.

'So what now, Sherlock?' I asked my young companion with sarcasm that was mixed with a hint of newfound respect for his abilities. Or had it all just been intuition on his part? It seemed that Juan had been right all along. He seemed to possess good instincts, much like Holmes did himself.

Juan just smiled a big toothy grin at me. 'You called me Sherlock.'

'Don't let it go to your head, youngster,' I told him bluntly. 'You were right about this one thing. Maybe. So what now?'

'I don't know.'

'Well, that's just fine,' I stammered, a bit overwhelmed by what we'd learned. What were we going to do about it? Wait for confirmation on the toxicology from Doctor Williams, and then his complaint to the medical board and the cops? But that might take days. What to do now? Then after thinking it over a bit, something came to me and I looked back at my young companion. 'I guess we should go and speak once again with the Adler family. See if we can find out anything more about that missing tin box.'

'Yeah, that sounds about right. I'm wondering what could be in that box,' Juan stated, almost in a dreamy voice.

'Yeah,' I repeated, catching his vibe. 'Me too.'

We said our goodbyes to Doctor Williams and left the city morgue, asking him to call me when he got the toxicology back and made his official statement. I didn't have a cell phone, being one of the last holdouts against the e-universe, so I gave him my phone number at home and the one at the store. He told me he'd give me a call once he found out anything new.

6

That Missing Tin Box

Joseph Adler's family proved not to be much help to us, as we had expected. They were elderly grandparents who had raised young Joseph the best they were able. They just lived in different worlds. With Joe's parents dead, and him being an only child, the link to his past and his family had been decisively cut, unless there were some family papers or records that could help us. I wondered about that. There must be something, somewhere? We needed to find that tin box.

Juan and I were allowed to look through the house again, this time not only up in the attic but through the entire home. We looked everywhere. Juan was especially good at finding little nooks and crannies that would have made great hiding places for the box. However there was no tin box anywhere to be found; nor had it suddenly reappeared up in the attic, as I had hoped it might. I surmised that perhaps the Adlers had hidden it themselves, for whatever reason I could not determine. But as I soon learned, I did not need to fear on that score. They had no hidden agenda; they were the plain folk they appeared to be. After talking with them quite carefully, I could tell the Adlers were being straight with us.

We searched the rest of the house and the basement. Nothing. We were finally even allowed into Joseph's bedroom, and Juan and I gave it a thorough search. I was rather surprised and somewhat delighted in a Holmesian way to see Juan take out a large magnifying glass and examine the carpet minutely for any trace of evidence. I had no idea what he was looking for, but he seemed to have focused on something. Then he looked over the bedding and eventually moved to the tops of the bureau and desk, giving all of it the most minute observation with his lens.

'Well, Juan?' I asked, my impatience fairly bursting as I intently watched him move about the room examining every tiny seemingly insignificant item. He ruminated over every speck of dross and meaningless crumb of dust. I really was reminded of the great detective hot upon a case. Juan had a certain affinity for Holmes, that much was plain to me; seemingly channeling his inner Sherlock.

I continued to watch, transfixed as my young friend intensified his search, doing a rather lengthy examination of Adler's room. Then he moved on to the closet, going through the young man's clothes, finally shouting in delight, 'Ah, ha! What's this?'

'What?' I blurted, watching him look through the drawers of the bureau now; but Juan did not answer me. Was he ignoring me? He was obviously obsessed and in complete mental focus now. I was beginning to understand just how poor Watson felt at times with Holmes.

My young friend continued his search. 'Juan?' I asked softly, but he still did not answer. It was exasperating; I was not one used to being ignored like this. Then I hit upon another tack and allowed myself a broad grin, for I would use the great detective's own name to gain my friend's attention. 'What have you found, *Holmes*?'

Juan suddenly froze; he had heard me for sure. Then his head slowly titled towards me with an almost insectoid precision, his eyes sharply centered upon my own, and he allowed a sly grin, finally answering me with, 'Very good, *Watson*.'

'I think I liked it better when you called me *Viejo*,' I muttered, channeling my inner grouch.

'I've found some interesting hints, some tell-tale signs,' Juan replied enthusiastically.

I was intrigued. 'Can you tell me what you've found?'

'There's cocaine residue on the top of the bureau. Joseph Alder was most certainly a drug user, and cocaine seemed to be the drug of choice, as they say, for him.'

'Cocaine? But he OD'ed from a heroin overdose.'

'That's correct,' Juan replied sharply.

'Then you must be wrong. I myself saw the tracks on the boy's arm when he came into my store to sell me the magazine,' I said, recalling what I had seen days before. Was the kid a cocaine addict, or was he given a hot shot of heroin? Or was he an addict of both drugs? Perhaps he just shot up cocaine? I'd heard that some people did that. I was perplexed.

'Old tracks or new?' Juan asked me sharply.

I looked up at my young friend. He had me there. The tracks didn't look recent, but what did I know? I was no expert. I did remember I saw no bruising, no open sores; there seemed to be no dried blood that I noticed. 'I'm not sure. I guess they could've been old marks, but maybe he was shooting up in another part of his body. It's consistent with what we've found out about him so far.'

'Well, *Viejo*, I know for sure that they were old tracks,' Juan said confidently. 'The night you met me and my friends by the fire and I told you Adler was in that crack house, he was there doing a coke deal, not using heroin. I think someone held him down, or struck him, and then gave him a hot shot of heroin, like the doctor told us.'

'Really?' I asked, shaking my head. It wasn't that I doubted what Juan had said — but why? 'Why kill the kid?'

'Why, indeed?' Juan answered me with a cryptic Sherlockian tone he had recently acquired, which I was beginning to dislike exceedingly. 'He knew something. Something about someone. Oh well, we shall see what the evidence tells me. There are some other things his bedroom tells me. Minor stuff, admittedly, but it may be of some significance.'

'Can you tell me what you've discovered?'

'Trivial hints, as Holmes might say,' Juan said rather mysteriously. 'Come on; we're done here. I think we need to see Andrea Tatos — she was Joseph Adler's on-again, off-again girl, and she might have some answers for us.'

'How do you know about her, Juan?' I asked, looking at my young friend curiously. He seemed a font of surprises.

'From school. We hung with the same group for a while and she mentioned Joseph Adler a few times to me; that's how I knew about his grandparents and that the dude was into some interesting stuff.'

I nodded, following Juan out of the bedroom. We thanked the Adlers for all their help. The elderly couple missed Joseph dearly, but his demise was not much of a shock for them. We didn't mention to them that we thought Joseph had been murdered, as I thought it was much too early for that. We did tell them we'd try to get to the bottom of what happened, however, and they said it was nice that someone cared.

* * *

Andrea Tatos lived about ten blocks over in the new section of Dorchester. It was an upscale neighborhood with larger, more luxurious homes. It amazed me how just ten blocks in distance could mean the difference between a world of dire poverty, violence and hopelessness and one of upper-class privilege and what could seemingly ensure a successful and happy life. Geography matters.

On the drive over, I decided to ask Juan

about events in his own personal past that I'd had on my mind since he'd first mentioned them to me so sparingly. I asked him what had happened to that good kid I had given that Holmes book to so long ago. What had happened to him and his family? Why had he left school? I know he didn't want to talk about these things, but I felt I had to at least make an effort to ask him; to show an interest.

'I'm not being nosy,' I said with care, 'but if you want to talk about things, well, we're friends, aren't we? I'm an older guy, and I've been through a lot; maybe I can help you make sense of some things.'

'Why?' Juan blurted, looking at me from across the passenger seat of my old Chevy with suspicion. It wasn't like him to be like that. 'What do you care?'

I looked back at him hard. 'Well, I give a damn, Juan! I liked that kid who came into my store years ago, and I like the young man he's become now. If you don't want to talk about any of it, I'll understand — but don't you think for a goddamn minute that I'm being nosy. It's just because I care about you, kid.'

Juan glared at me but said nothing. I guess he was thinking it through. I nodded and continued the short drive to the Tatos residence in silence.

Juan finally said, '*Viejo*, it's a long story, and a hard one for me to talk about.'

'I got time — all the time in the world for you, if you want to talk about it,' I told him in a warm tone. 'It's up to you.'

Juan sighed. 'I don't know where to begin. I don't understand how you can be a kid and you think everything is going great in your life and then suddenly before you know it, everything turns to dust. How can things go to hell so fast? Why does that happen?'

I didn't know how to answer that. I hardly knew what to say, and began wondering if I had opened a wound better left closed, or if I had gotten in over my head. I was no therapist. I just went with my gut. I said, 'Juan, I'm not that smart, but I do know that you're not the only one this has happened to in his life. Things fall apart. Sometimes it just happens. I'm sure none of it was your fault, and it's nothing to feel embarrassed about.'

He nodded slowly, thinking deeply.

'You can start at the beginning.'

'Yeah, I guess that's the way to do it. Like I would tell it to Holmes?'

'Yes, that's it, tell it just like you were telling it to Sherlock Holmes,' I said with a wry grin.

'Or to Doctor Watson?'

I nodded. 'Sure, Juan. Doctor Watson was a good listener.'

My young friend smiled. 'Well, *Viejo*, when I first met you, when you gave me that Holmes book, that gift really changed my life. For the better. It made me start to think about a lot of things. One of them was why someone I didn't even know would give me a gift like that. Why were you being so nice to me? At first I was suspicious, you know? What does this old guy want? Who is he? But you didn't want anything. I never came back into your store. There was no reason for what you did that I could see then, other than you are just a decent person. I know that now. It makes me feel better to know that there are really some people like that in the world.'

I looked at him, taken aback, and said simply, 'I'm not all that decent, but I do try to be, I really do, but too often I fall short. Anyway, I could see you wanted that book real bad but couldn't pay for it. I knew you had no money. That was okay too. Being a good bookman means more than just selling books for money; it means getting the right book to the right person, and if that means sometimes giving a book away as a gift, well then, I think there's no better gift one can give.'

Juan nodded. 'Your gift made me think about a lot of things in my life back then. I also read that book and loved every word written there. I became a Sherlock Holmes fanatic. I must have read that book five times. Then I read other Sherlock Holmes books, then a lot of other books. Soon I was becoming a real reader, and I noticed it was also making me smarter. I mean, I was learning things, questioning things . . . and I liked it. And what's more, I was learning *how* to think. You know, like critically. Books did that for me, and your simple gift was the impetus of all that.'

My eyes misted over for a moment but I said nothing.

'Learning how to think critically was the greatest gift I ever received from books; from reading,' Juan added proudly.

I nodded. That was good to hear.

'And from you,' he continued.

I smiled. 'Well, thank you. But it's not me, it's the books. Anyway, you're correct about critical thinking. I am afraid it is a lost art these days.'

'You sure got that right! When you really start thinking critically about things, seeing all the bullshit for what it is, you ask yourself a lot of questions; some of them not very nice, some of them about yourself, your life, your choices. And when you start asking questions, they just naturally lead to more questions.'

I laughed happily. 'Boy, are you in trouble.'

'Right you are!' Juan told me sharply. 'The books, all that reading, helped me to open my eyes, *Viejo*, to see what was around me; *why* it was around me. I asked so many questions. Maybe too many.'

'You can never ask too many questions,' I told him.

Juan was quiet for a moment. I turned the corner and drove down Drummond Avenue, where Andrea Tatos's house was located. I parked the car and shut off the ignition, but neither of us got out of the vehicle just yet.

Juan continued, 'I thought my life was so good, and maybe it was at that time, since everything seemed fine. My mother and father were together; we had money and a nice house. I had a great mom and pops and a lovely younger sister. It was all about to crash down, *Viejo*. It was all phony, built on quicksand. I found out my parents had problems. Pops was a cheater going out on Mom and he made his money selling drugs. Mom was a drunk. My sister — she was hit by a car and died. Then my mother suicided out; she just couldn't take it any longer. Not soon after, a rival drug dealer took out my pops. Shot him dead right in front of our house. Now they're all dead, all gone, but

I loved them all. My mom and pops. My little sister. All dead. I really miss them . . . '

'Oh, Juan, I'm so sorry,' I said softly, gripping his shoulder tightly.

'Old news now, *Viejo. No problemo*. So I found myself alone, but at least I had the books and I kept reading. Somehow they helped me. The stories, the characters, they were all heroic stories that I read, with real heroes overcoming seemingly insurmountable odds. Like Holmes and Watson. It was . . . well, the books inspired me to cope with my dark days and to overcome them. I'd dropped out of school by then but I'm back in now, taking classes. I still hang out with my boys on the street corner — I've known them for years — but we're not a gang; we're just friends, like brothers. I think of them as my Baker Street Irregulars — Fat Jose, Enrique, and Pedro. We hang together and try to keep the drug dealers away from our block. We keep the little kids away from those people, from that house. We won't allow them to go in there. We were on duty. That's what we were doing when you came over to us the other night — keeping our eyes on that house so we could keep the local kids away — 'specially the little ones.'

'Why didn't you just call the cops?' I asked simply, perhaps too simply.

Juan just laughed. 'You are quite naive for a wise old man, *Viejo*.'

I was going to say something against that, then realized he might just be right.

'Perhaps things work differently in your part of town,' Juan said firmly. 'That could be it. But this is the drug spot in the West Side, and things work their own way here.'

'I see,' I said demurely.

Juan smiled. 'No problem. That's life, that's just the way it is. It's not as bad as the war zone on the East Side. That's really bad turf. Anyway, I've called the cops on the people in that drug house before, spoke to detectives, but they wouldn't act. I couldn't figure it out at first. At first I figured it had to be that the cops were paid off, but then I was told the police had a CI in there.'

'A confidential informant?' I asked, amazed.

'Yes; at least that was the word. But I could never get a definite answer on that either; no one would tell me anything for certain. Who was I, after all? Just some street kid asking a lot of nosy questions and maybe causing trouble. But that CI just might've been Joseph Adler.'

'Damn!' I blurted. 'That sure changes things and makes everything more complicated.'

'If it's true,' Juan cautioned.

'If it's true.'

'So what now?'

'Now we go to speak to Adler's girlfriend, or whatever she was to him,' I said, getting ready to get out of my Chevy.

Juan put his hand on my arm and looked at me squarely. 'Thanks for listening. You know, about my personal stuff. I never told anyone those things before. It's good to get it off my chest.'

I nodded. 'I'm glad I could be here for you. No problem, Juan. Do you think the person who killed Adler was also a drug dealer?'

'Yes, for sure.'

Then a thought came to me. 'Do you

think the drug dealer who killed Adler could be the same one who murdered your father?'

Juan looked at me in shock, obviously stunned by the realization. 'I honestly never thought of that.'

'Just a wild hunch I had. I figured I'd mention it. It's probably nothing,' I added.

'No, I don't think it could be true. It couldn't be the same person. Many years separate the two murders, and my father was shot with a gun, while Adler was an OD done on purpose. Very different.'

'I'm sure you're right. Now let's go and talk with this Andrea Tatos and see what we can learn from her.'

'*Si, Viejo*, that's a very good idea. Let's go.'

7

Andrea Tells Us What She Knows

Andrea Tatos was a Dorchester High School senior who told us she knew Joseph Adler for the last year of his life. She told us they had gone out a few times but that it was nothing serious. She didn't know if Adler had a thing with any other girls at school. Probably not.

'He did have some problems with a gang on the East Side who sold him coke. Joe seemed to love his cocaine; at least that's what I thought at the time,' Andrea said with a faint smile, remembering. 'He was actually very generous with it. He turned me on many times. All my friends too. It made Joe a really popular guy, but I never saw him do it himself. Strange, ain't it? He was a nice guy too, and good-looking, so the coke was just an added plus for us, you know?'

She looked at Juan when she spoke. He

just replied, 'Yeah, I know. Popular guy.'

'Yes. You knew him, Juan?' Andrea said, curious now.

'A little, but I never hung with him,' Juan stated.

'I didn't either, really. I don't think Joe ever really hung with any specific crowd at all. He made the rounds. He was very outgoing, but a strange guy. It was almost as if he was on some kind of mission.'

I looked at Juan and I could see his eyes blazing with intense thoughts. 'What do you mean, mission?' I asked softly.

'I don't know, exactly.' Andrea looked at me, smiling wanly. 'It was like Joe had no place of his own, no real friends. Like he was a lost soul. It was sad, really. A lot of girls liked him for various reasons — some just for the coke, you know — but he always seemed to stay to himself. I knew he wasn't gay or anything like that. It was just that he stayed apart. Like he was alone, afraid to get too close to anyone. Or maybe afraid to let anyone get too close to him. He was into some stuff. I know he was buying and selling a lot of coke. He was big into it, but he didn't seem to use it himself. That was weird too. I think maybe that was his mission, strange as it seems — trying to make an in with the drug dealers for some reason.'

'He did heroin at one time,' I said. 'I saw the track marks on his arm. Can you tell me anything about that?'

'Maybe he did, but that was before I knew him. He didn't do that when I knew him. I think he experimented with it for a while, then dropped it. Or he got clean. I don't know for sure. I don't think he really liked H at all,' she told us.

'He just dropped H, just like that?' Juan asked in wonder.

'Yes, that's the way I heard it. He got clean. Joe was like that — he had great self-control,' Andrea stated. 'He never went near heroin again, and after a while I think he left coke too.'

'You heard he died from a heroin overdose?' I asked Andrea.

'Yes, I heard. That just can't be,' she said sharply. 'No way!'

'What can you tell us about that East Side gang and did he owe them money? Who are they?' I asked carefully now. 'We won't mention your name.'

'You're not the cops, so why do you care?' Andrea asked, suddenly suspicious.

'No we're not the cops, but we think Joe was murdered. We want to find out who did it. Don't you?' Juan asked her bluntly.

Andrea nodded and finally said, 'Yeah, all right. Those guys, they're the usual crowd down there. There are three or four gangs that control turf on the East Side. Joe bought from them. Maybe he owed them money. I'm not really sure.'

'Who are they?' Juan insisted. I knew he was trying to pin her down and make her give us some names.

'You know them, Juan. I'm not giving away any secrets here,' Andrea said, looking intently at my young friend. 'The 8th Street Locos run by Robert X, the Green Hill Gang run by Crazy Zee, and there's The Dollarz Boyz, and then Riomondo. Probably a few others.'

I nodded. It seemed like it was an endless group of dealers and distributors. It was Juan who got down to the real point about it all.

'And out of all of them, who is their supplier, Andrea? Give us the name of the man who runs it all,' Juan said in an effort to pry the info out of her.

The girl looked hard at my young friend. 'You know that too, Juan. It has to be only one person, the top man, and that top man has to be Charles St. Simon. Joe told me he's the man who calls all the shots in the East Side when it comes to the gangs and drugs.'

'Joe told you?' I blurted.

'Yes; he mentioned it once, then told me to forget he'd ever said it. That was a long time ago. Of course, these days all the druggies know who the main man is.'

Juan nodded. 'Just as I figured.'

'I heard of him,' I said curiously and a bit surprised, 'but not in this capacity. He donates to the poor; he was even given an award by the mayor last year.'

Juan just laughed, and he looked at Andrea and she joined him. It was like some secret youth code, things they knew about, that I being older did not.

'He's been around for a long time, Juan,' Andrea said. Then she looked hard at my young companion. 'Since your own father was working for him . . . and passed on.'

'Your father worked for him?' I asked Juan in obvious shock. He hadn't mentioned *that* to me.

'Yeah,' Juan admitted coldly, but said no more about it.

I dropped my questions about that for now. Instead I said, 'Charles St. Simon? I can't believe it. He's a big supporter of the Police Athletic League; he gives money to the poor and donates food to the hungry. I heard only good things about him. I remember him from my working days; my college even bestowed him with an honorary degree.'

Juan just shook his head in exasperation.

Andrea looked at me and smiled grimly. 'A degree? What was it for?'

I swallowed hard. 'Urban Ecology, or something like that. I don't know exactly what it means, maybe nothing, but he sure was happy to get the accolades from my college administration. And they were happy to give him the degree. I heard he gave a large donation — I guess he bought his degree.'

'Now you know how he paid for it,' Andrea said bitterly. Then she looked at us longingly. 'Are you going to find out who killed Joe Adler? He was a good guy and he did not OD on H. He stayed away from it and was getting out of drugs altogether.'

'Yes,' Juan answered her firmly, 'we're looking into it.'

'Good. Then if there's anything else I can do to help you, let me know,' Andrea told us. She gave us a sad smile. 'I liked Joe. I think he was a tortured soul. I wonder why.'

'I'd like to know that myself,' I said softly. 'Well, thanks, Andrea.'

Then Juan and I left the house and headed back to my car.

* * *

Once Juan and I were seated in the less than luxurious comfort of my old beater of a Chevy Aveo, we got down to talking serious business.

'We got a big job ahead of us, *Viejo*,'

Juan told me as I put the key in the ignition and started up my car. I was pleasantly surprised that it started up right on my first try. It's nice to have a car that you can rely on. I was behind the wheel but didn't pull out yet, as I had no idea what to do next and where I was headed. I looked over at Juan. 'What's our next move?'

'That's a good question, *Watson*,' Juan answered, showing a mischievous grin.

'Stop calling me Watson,' I growled back at him.

'Okay, *Viejo*.'

'I don't really like that *Viejo* stuff either. I'm not that old, you know?'

'Not that old? You're more than three times my age. I hate to break it to you, but that's *old*.'

I grumbled but said nothing. Grumbled like an old man. Dammit, maybe I was . . . Juan looked at me and laughed joyfully. 'You're a good guy, though — Watson, *Viejo*, Professor, *Jefe*.'

Now he was calling me all the nicknames he had created for me. I sighed and put the Aveo in gear and drove off. I guess

I did know where we were going next, but I didn't want to think about it.

'You want to go out to the East Side, don't you?'

'Don't you?' Juan asked.

'No, but I guess it's the next logical place we have to look.'

'Yes,' Juan answered firmly. Then he asked me, 'You have your revolver?'

'Yes.'

'We might have need of it.'

I sighed deeply. This was getting deep. I drove my old Chevy out of my spot and headed towards the East Side.

8

On the East Side

I drove carefully over the East River Bridge on into the East Side of Dorchester. It was another world out here. It was a land full of projects and the poor, gangs and turf wars. The cops were not available most times, and even the fire department hesitated to answer calls out here. And with good reason — cops and firemen were often prime targets for gang snipers from high-rise project windows and rooftops.

It was a different world here from anything I had ever encountered in my academic book world. I realized right away that Juan had been correct. I *was* naïve. I had led a sheltered life — a good one, but definitely sheltered. Thank God for that! I thought. But as I drove further into the morass that was the East Side, I realized this place was a dark world different even from where my young friend Juan Marcano and the murdered Joseph Adler had lived. Life on our side of the river *could* be hard, but life on the East Side of the river was *always* hard. Every minute. And violent. And too often short-lived. *Deadly* described it perfectly.

I drove carefully over the bridge, and we were now fully into what looked like another world that was different from my own on the other side of the river.

'Keep your gun handy, *Viejo*,' Juan cautioned. I could see his eyes scanning the area all around us furiously. 'We're in the meat grinder now. The War Zone. That's what they call it. And keep your head down. Snipers.'

I nodded. Snipers? What was this, downtown Baghdad? *Meat grinder* was the slang term out here for the East Side or War Zone, and it seemed to describe the place most effectively. I drove down Tumar Street. The houses there were all gutted, fire-bombed years earlier and never rebuilt. Multi-story projects loomed over the area like giant monsters ready to devour everyone within sight. Inside them I knew lived some real monsters — but also many innocent victims trapped by circumstances who were virtually prisoners of war. It was as grim and dark as Tolkien's Mordor.

'So what's the plan, Sherlock?' I asked Juan caustically.

He looked at me boldly, thought about it and smiled. I figured up to that moment he'd not really thought things through that far, but I was wrong. He wasn't perplexed, he was fearful. I could see the signs of impending danger in his face.

'What?' I stammered, nervous myself now, wondering what had him so spooked.

'Keep driving. We go to the top, *Viejo*. We have to see Charles St. Simon himself. Question him, and see what we can find out.'

I looked at my young companion like he had finally lost his mind. This was his great plan? Come here to speak to the headmaster of all criminal monsters? The worst of the worst! The man who had probably ordered the murder of Joseph Adler? That was his plan? Were we just going to drive up and speak to St. Simon about it? And of course, he would see us immediately and tell us everything we wanted to know? Yeah! And Juan said *I* was naïve!

I finally said, 'I think this is crazy! What makes you think he'll even see us, much less answer any of our questions?'

'That's true. He may just have us shot on sight.'

I laughed nervously. 'You're kidding, right?'

'Actually, *Viejo*, I've never been more serious. The truth is we're taking a big risk coming here, but you have to take risks to get anywhere in life.'

'Perhaps he'll know something about the missing box?' I asked.

'I don't know. I can't see how, but it can't hurt to ask.'

I swallowed hard, my nerves jittery now, but I guess we had to go through with it. We had to do something. I just wish we didn't have to do this, but I knew we must. For Joseph Adler. *Dammit!* I only hoped Juan would be able to keep his cool about this, because there was some possibility St. Simon might have been responsible for his own father's death. Juan had already told me he didn't buy that story, but I was concerned the kid just might change his mind; then his temper could blow up and that would end things badly for us both. Like getting us made dead real quick.

'You okay with this? St. Simon, well, he may have — you know? Can you keep it cool? I mean under control?' I asked him, suddenly concerned that the lad might lose it in a direct or angry confrontation with St. Simon.

'I'm always cool!' Juan told me with a bold, confident grin.

'Yeah, that's what they all say just before they go *loco*. Just don't try anything with St. Simon — if we can even get to see him, and that's not a sure thing. What's to stop you from jumping him and killing him right there?'

'I'm a professional, *Viejo*. You hurt me when you talk like that. I am not here to avenge my pops, but to get evidence for the murder of Joseph Adler, and maybe get a lead on that missing tin box,' Juan said seriously, feigning that his pride was hurt. 'Come on, let's see what St. Simon can tell us. One murder at a time, okay?'

I nodded as I continued driving slowly down the rutted streets, passing more burned-out homes and graffiti-ridden walls full of gang sign, over to a large open area surrounded by a high brick wall with a large lonely house atop a hill of well-tended gardens. It was St. Simon's home, office, headquarters, whatever. It had once been a part of the neighborhood, but all the neighboring buildings had been burned down, the people run off, the land sold, and now it all belonged to Charles St. Simon — his own walled fortress and estate built in the middle of utter mayhem.

I drove up slowly, careful and scared. There were young men with guns everywhere I looked. As we got close, they aimed their weapons at us in warning. I continued driving closer, very slowly but not too slowly so it looked like we might be on a drive-by shooting. We didn't need that. Juan instructed me as I drove.

'Lose the revolver, *Viejo*,' he told me suddenly.

'But you told me to take it?' I reacted in surprise, but I was relieved nevertheless. 'Not here, not with these people. Get rid of it now.'

I nodded, quickly took the .38 out of my jacket pocket, and shoved it into the glove compartment. I never liked that gun anyway, but now I realized we'd have to go in to see St. Simon unarmed, and that didn't make me feel very safe, not with so many armed thugs visible. That was, if we were allowed in to see the big man at all. They might just shoot us on sight. However, getting *inside* wasn't what I was really concerned about just then — getting *out* was what I was really worried about.

I parked the car and we sat there silent and unmoving, our hands on the dashboard. Four heavily armed black guys came over towards us. They were huge steroid-manufactured goons ready for trouble; hoping for it, in fact. I looked nervously at Juan and shrugged, not sure at all now that this had been such a good idea. He just gave me a wry grin, knowing we were going into the maw of the beast by seeking to speak with St. Simon.

'What do you want here?' the largest and meanest-looking of the quartet of brutes demanded. I noticed his right hand was heavily wrapped in bandages and idly wondered just what might have happened to that hand. He held a weapon in his other hand; and while he didn't point it at us, his three companions did. Right at our heads. I gulped nervously, looking at Juan.

He just smiled at me. 'Come on, *Viejo*. You want to live forever? Go ahead, talk to them.'

'Why me?'

'That's the plan,' he told me simply.

'That's the plan?' I stammered.

'Yes, now get to work.'

I shook my head in exasperation and abject fear. But I tried not to show my nervousness as I looked at the lead thug and said boldly, 'We need to speak with Mr. St. Simon.'

He just laughed derisively. 'Not possible, old man. Now why don't you and the kid turn your old heap around and head far away from the East Side. Or be prepared to be buried here. I knows you're not from around here. This is East Side territory.'

I tried not to shiver in fear and looked at Juan in the passenger seat beside me. He just smiled, whispering, 'You're doing fine, *Viejo*. Just fine.'

Well that certainly makes me feel better, I thought to myself. We had planned in advance that I would do most of the talking, but I didn't like it. I don't know why Juan wanted it that way. He told me it would work better. I had no idea why. I wasn't sure it was such a good idea, but I was committed now. I had no choice but to continue with our plan.

I noticed the cell phone on the belt of the guy with the bandaged hand, so I got an idea and looked up at him seriously and said, 'I know your boss will want to speak to us. Get him on that cell phone and tell him we're here to speak to him about the Joseph Adler murder.'

The thug leader scrunched up his face looking at us in anger, then he rubbed his bandaged hand. He was really annoyed at us now. I could see we were bothering him, and I thought he was going to have his boys give us a whooping, but then he seemed to think better of it. He rubbed his injured hand and gave me a sharp look. There was a hint of concern, even curiosity in his face suddenly.

'Joe Adler, eh?' he said sharply, thinking it over. 'That was an OD.'

'That's what you think. I know Mr. St. Simon will be interested in the news we have for him about it.'

The thug thought that over again and then reluctantly got on his cell phone and spoke to someone in the house — most certainly *not* St. Simon himself, but another thug who was now relaying the message to the big man. We waited.

Juan looked at the four armed henchmen surrounding us, their weapons still leveled at us and just itching to pull those triggers and make hamburger meat out of us. It was a sobering feeling, and a trickle of nervous sweat ran down my back. What if this plan of his didn't work? What if these goons took us out and shot us? Juan was right, things like that happened all the time out here on the East Side. It could happen to us now. We were no one special. We had no protection. No one even knew we were here. I tried to hold down my panic.

I steeled myself, confronting the thug. 'Well?'

'Hold on,' the lead thug told me. He was still waiting for a response from the house.

'Be patient. He'll see us. I know he will,' Juan told me, oozing confidence.

I nodded, wondering how he could be so positive in such a negative situation. Juan just smiled back. I felt like we were about to be taken out and shot any moment. My nerves were jumping.

The lead thug's cell rang and he quickly answered it. He suddenly got a two-word message that sounded like garbled static, but it said simply, 'Bring them.'

The lead thug looked at us with a death's head smile, showing off his impressive grillwork. He looked scary to me, but all these guys looked scary to me.

'Okay, both of you get out of the car and stand for a pat-down. Any weapons on you?' he asked us wickedly.

'No,' I replied truthfully.

'No,' Juan repeated when the thug looked over at him harshly.

'If we find anything on you, we'll shoot you down dead. That's the rules. No one brings a weapon into the house when they see the boss. Now stand for a pat-down.'

It was a good thing Juan had me leave my revolver in the car. These were serious thugs, dangerous and violent, and they wouldn't hesitate to kill either of us if we crossed them. Having a weapon on us when we tried to see their boss could mean a death sentence. The only thing keeping us alive so far was that St. Simon wanted to see us, obviously to learn what we had to say about Adler. I only hoped after we talked to the crime master that we'd be able to walk out of there alive.

They patted us down all over, then one of the thugs announced, 'Okay, drop 'em!'

'Drop what?' I asked confused and surprised.

'Your drawers,' the thug ordered, letting me feel the cold barrel of his weapon on my neck. 'Strip search. Drop your pants.'

'Out here? Out in the open?' I blurted, angry, embarrassed. The thugs were just laughing. Juan nudged me, indicating I should do as I was told.

'You're kidding, right?' I asked the thug, but one look at his grim face and I knew that he was not. I muttered softly, 'It's cold out here.'

He laughed. 'Too bad. Now drop 'em!'

I did. So did Juan. We stripped to our underwear, and they went over us by hand and with metal detectors and wands. It was worse than being at the airport. It was also bad because it was all happening outside on the street. It was cold, really cold, and embarrassing. People were watching, pointing, and . . . laughing.

'My God, what the hell are they looking for?' I asked Juan in alarm. Their search was very thorough, one might even say too thorough.

He shook his head. 'Poison pills, razor blades, shivs, you know.'

I did not know. I was ashamed; I'd

never been treated like that before. I felt so violated. The thugs only laughed and made rude comments. They were having fun at our expense. Mostly my expense.

One of the thugs made fun of my knobby knees. Then he called me *chicken-legs* and made clucking sounds. He and all his buddies laughed wildly. I was highly offended and embarrassed, but they were all laughing, so now I was getting cranky. In spite of things, I couldn't help blurting out, 'Just you wait until you're 80 and see if you don't look any better. If any of you live that long!'

The thugs all laughed even more at that. They seemed to find my remarks very amusing, which rankled me even more.

Juan looked at me sharply and whispered, '*Viejo*, you're only 62. How come you told that guy you're 80?'

'Give him something to think about,' I replied in a low growl.

'Ah . . . ' Juan whispered, giving me a sly wink. 'Psychological warfare. I like it.'

'You two come on,' one of the thugs announced, waving at us to get dressed and stand by the wall. He had given us a most thorough pat-down and body search, though Juan told me that it beat being shot and killed on the spot. I reluctantly had to agree with him. That seemed to be the alternative for noncompliance.

'They pass, Reggie,' the thug growled to the guy in charge.

'You sure, Tyrone?' the leader called Reggie insisted.

'Sure; they're clean. I'd stake my life on it,' Tyrone replied calmly.

'You are,' Reggie informed him coldly.

I looked from Juan to Tyrone, then back to Reggie. These guys were serious. I began to sweat again as Juan and I dressed and stood against the wall as we had been told to do. Waiting.

'Okay, take four men and escort these two up to the big house to see the boss. Ahmad will be there waiting for you with the reception party,' Reggie ordered Tyrone.

Tyrone gathered three other armed thugs and escorted us through the walled gate that surrounded the estate where

Charles St. Simon lived. The house was a mansion, like some old southern plantation home, set smack in the midst of all the death and decay of the East Side war zone. It looked like the dark lord's castle on Mount Doom in Mordor from *The Lord of The Rings*, only this dark lord was more like Professor Moriarty, though a lot more real and deadly.

9

St. Simon's Creed

Juan and I were led upwards towards the spacious grounds where the big house sat atop the hill. The grounds were well manicured, mostly in the stylized beauty of intricate and well-kept Japanese gardens. It was most disconcerting and incongruous for me to see this abundance of luxury and wealth in what was a cesspool of East Side poverty and decay. But then again, Charles St. Simon probably told the locals he was raising the property values by locating his massive pile in their midst — doing it for their own good. Whether they believed it or not, they knew to keep their mouths shut if they knew what was good for them. St. Simon ruled here on the East Side; all the gangs in the War Zone worked for him or paid him a fee to operate. Any freelancers were found dead in the East River, bloated floaters the cops fished out of the cold waters with no one ever having seen a thing. No one ever talked.

'It's unbelievable,' Juan whispered to me in awe. My young friend had never seen the likes of this before except in movies or on TV. It was like the palace in *Scarface* where Al Pacino as Tony Montana lived. The gardens were large and actually glorious. The trees shielded the area, as well as an amazing Olympic-sized swimming pool. Around the pool and in the water Juan and I could see a bevy of young bikini-clad beauties of all shapes, sizes, and colors enjoying the sun, as well as drinks and drugs, all brought over to them by a brace of waiters. Armed waiters. A few men stood around, armed guards no doubt, and some others dressed in expensive suits, perhaps guests of the big man or business associates.

'How can they lay out there in the October chill . . . ?'

'Heated pool, Juan. The entire back yard must be heated. Heat radiates from filaments in the cement, from the walls, keeps it warm here year round,' I told him, amazed at the utter luxury.

'Damn!' Juan muttered. 'That's the life!'

I shrugged and looked at Juan. It was just like out of the movies. We were brought across the gardens and passed the pool and the beauties therein. Ah, if I was just 20 years younger . . .

'*Viejo?*' Juan asked — and never did I hate that appellation so much as just then. 'These women are fantastic! St. Simon lives like Hugh Hefner did years ago at the Playboy Mansion.'

'Except Hef didn't murder people to get where he is,' I reminded my young friend in a low voice I hoped our guards could not hear. 'Don't be too impressed by what this murderous thug has created here.'

'I'm not, *Jefe*, believe me,' Juan whispered back to me as we were led through the large oak doors into the big house. But we were impressed. We noticed armed guards all around us, their weapons trained upon us every moment. I had no doubts that these men, St. Simon's inner sanctum guards, had military training and knew their business. They looked it. They'd spray us with bullets if we posed any sign of danger.

'Walk more lightly here, Juan, and watch your words,' I cautioned.

'Yes,' Juan answered, noting we were not in Kansas anymore, nor even Dorchester.

'Follow me,' a new guard told us. He had taken over operations from Tyrone and his boys. I assume this was the house commander, a guy who I found out later was named Ahmad. He and his team led us into a large and bright garden room in the back of the house. It was actually quite nice. Large windows let in massive amounts of sunlight to shine upon a bevy of exotic plants and flowers. It was a lovely garden room. The smell from the flowers was intoxicating. We were led further inside. The room was presently empty. So was my font of ideas. Now that we were in his house and soon to speak to the man, I began to panic, wondering what I would actually say to Charles St. Simon that would not get us killed!

Ahmad ordered us to sit in the chairs

over at a white garden table, then he left us. Juan and I were alone now. Waiting. Seconds seemed to pass like hours.

'So what are you going to tell him, *Viejo*?' Juan suddenly asked me, as though the thought had just occurred to him — and maybe it had.

I was startled a bit by his words, and looked at my young companion carefully. 'Tell him? What am I going to tell him? I'm not quite sure.'

'You have to say something,' he whispered. That was Juan, just trying to be helpful.

'I know. I'm thinking.'

'So you have no plan?' Juan asked.

'Not really. Do you? After all, this was your idea.'

Juan shrugged. 'We'll just have to play it by ear then.'

That didn't sound so good, and I told him so.

'Then there's always Plan B.'

'I'm afraid to ask about that one, Juan.'

'Then don't.'

I sighed with deep exasperation as the door at the end of the room suddenly opened and a man entered. He was a tall, lean black man with a shaved head. The dome of his head actually shone. He had a pleasant face but stern bearing, and nice white teeth that showed a big bright smile. He let us see that smile now as he walked closer to us. I knew he was nothing but a deadly shark.

'I'm Charles St. Simon. So you braved my guards to come here and see me. Who are you and what do you want?' he asked seriously, obviously a man whose time was extremely valuable, getting down to business right away as he came over to stand at the table across from us, watching us intently.

'Well, Mr. St. Simon . . . ' I said.

'First allow me to caution you before we begin. If this is some sort of lame assassination attempt, know that my sharpshooters have you in their sites at this very moment, and they never miss. Now please answer my questions. I repeat, who are you and what do you want?'

I sighed. 'My name is Thomas Jones. I'm a retired English professor from

Dorchester College. And this young man is Juan Marcano, a friend of mine.'

'You mentioned the death of Joseph Adler,' St. Simon asked curiously. 'You must be aware the police and the ME have determined his death was from a drug overdose. Heroin. An accident. Most unfortunate.'

'Yes, but we don't exactly buy that, Mr. St. Simon,' Juan stated boldly. 'We asked around, learned a few things, and we're sure that Adler was murdered. Is there anything you can tell us that could help us clear up his murder? Did he work for you?'

Charles St. Simon laughed. 'Are you the police? You have no jurisdiction in this situation.'

'We're not the police and we have no legal jurisdiction,' I answered firmly, 'but we're interested. The ME will soon determine the death to be a murder rather than what the police have termed to be just a standard run-of-the-mill drug OD. There's much more involved here than many people believe.'

'And why is that? Why should I even be

here listening to any of this nonsense? Your questions are offensive. Maybe I should have my men take you out of here — maybe have them teach you a lesson in manners as well?' St. Simon said, smiling with those pearly whites of his now, showing us his shark teeth.

I tamped down my fear and decided to play a hunch. 'Do you know anything about the tin dispatch box Joseph Adler had in his possession, sir?'

The effect on Charles St. Simon was instantaneous and rather amazing. His eyebrows shot up and his gaze shot to my face, his mouth tight and grim. I looked back at him and smiled. *Ah, seems I've hit a nerve*, I thought. I saw there was something there. Juan could see it too.

'How do you know about that box?' St. Simon demanded.

'That we know about it at all is enough for you to consider very carefully,' Juan added boldly.

St. Simon gave a careful and thoughtful look at Juan. 'And you have this box in your possession?'

Juan smiled back and began to speak,

but I put my hand upon his arm in a ceasing gesture. He looked at me, then back at St. Simon. 'Perhaps if you tell us how Joseph Adler died and why, we can help you locate that tin box,' I said. 'You seem to be interested in obtaining it, unless I am mistaken.'

St. Simon thought this over a bit, reluctantly nodded. It was a trade. Trades were something he could understand. I figured he was willing to trade to get something he wanted — after all, I knew and he knew, he could always have us killed later. So he seemed to like trades. 'Joseph Adler was a distributor of my product on the West Side,' St. Simon added, aware of what he was admitting but apparently unconcerned. He knew we were not wired. There was no danger to him from us or anything he told us. Anything he admitted to us, he could always deny later. I looked at Juan carefully, warning him with my eyes to tread lightly. We were entering deep waters here. People got killed for this kind of knowledge.

'You had him murdered?' I asked.

‘I didn’t say that. I had nothing to do with that. In fact, I’m rather upset that he was murdered. It was never in my plans. However, he took something of mine that I want back.’

‘I see,’ I said, trying to let the implications sink in. ‘Can I ask you what that might be?’

St. Simon looked at me hard, dangerous now. It seemed he had come to some decision and saw through our ruse. ‘So you don’t have the box. Then you’re wasting my time.’

‘We know where we can get it!’ Juan blurted quickly, saving the day and very likely our skins.

St. Simon thought about that for a moment, relaxed a bit, then suddenly nodded and said, ‘You can ask, but you’ll get no answer from me on that question.’

‘Fair enough, but what you seek is in that tin dispatch box,’ Juan stated quickly, not offering it as a question but as a statement of fact.

‘I believe so. I want that box. Unopened,’ St. Simon said. Then he asked us directly, ‘Do you have it or not?’

Juan and I did not reply right away. We were in a box ourselves just then and we knew it. It was a tight little box of our own making. If we lied and said we had the box, we were in the soup — he'd likely kill us and take it from us, or force us to bring it to him, perhaps keeping one of us as a hostage. If we admitted we didn't have it, we might be in danger as well. It was a mess, a no-win situation, that I feared could swirl out of control real quick.

St. Simon read our faces and gestures with a dark, grim look. 'You don't have it.'

'No,' I stated truthfully, hoping he'd buy my play. 'But I know where we can get it.'

The mobster looked at me suspiciously, then over at my young companion, and stared at him deeply. 'Your name is Juan Marcano. Your father was Alberto Marcano?'

'Yes,' Juan admitted softly. Both of us were now wondering if this was the very man who had killed his father years before.

'You know your father worked for me,'

St. Simon said in a stoic tone, admitting nothing more.

'I heard that,' Juan said simply. 'It was a long time ago. He sold drugs?'

'Yes, and he was good at it, but greedy.'

'Did you kill him?' Juan suddenly blurted, and I couldn't believe he'd let loose with a question like that. Not here and not now! It could mean a death sentence for us to get this man angry. I could see St. Simon was not amused. He centered his deadly snake-eyes upon me, then focused them upon Juan.

'No, it was a rival gang. We were at war. It was the old days before I had consolidated things here on the East Side, before I had brought peace,' St. Simon explained forcefully. This was a man not used to explaining his actions to anyone; a man, I wondered, who had brought peace — but at what price? 'Now, we are finished with our talk. I want that tin box, and I want you both to bring it to me, unopened. I want my property back. I want it now!'

Then Charles St. Simon got up to leave, walking away from us towards the door. Before he left he ordered his henchman, 'Ahmad, take them back to their car and see that they leave us, unhurt, for now.' Then he looked back at us fiercely. 'I want that box. Find it and bring it to me — or else!'

We both knew what 'or else' meant.

I took a deep nervous breath and Juan whipped beads of sweat from his forehead, then we quickly followed Ahmad out of the room. Tyrone and his goon squad escorted us out of the house, down the hill and finally over to my old Chevy. I was never so happy to be back in my car and drive away from a place in my life.

10

Two Detectives

I drove slowly, nervously, Juan and I each wrapped within our own dire thoughts. We'd discovered a lot of things, we now realized, but was any of it of actual use to us? The one thing we did know was that the most powerful criminal leader in Dorchester wanted what was in Joseph Adler's tin dispatch box. Or, to be more precise, Dr. John Watson's tin dispatch box. We both wondered what in the world could be in there that St. Simon would want so badly. It certainly couldn't be anything connected with Arthur Conan Doyle or Sherlock Holmes, as we'd originally supposed. It had to be something much darker and more deadly.

'He's scared,' Juan stated simply. 'I could see it in his face, his eyes. Nothing scares a guy like that, but he's scared about what's in that box.'

I nodded. It certainly seemed that at least he was seriously concerned. That very fact interested me very much also — and now it scared me as well.

I drove back to my bookshop, where Juan and I could finally sit down quietly and in safety to plan our next move. We were in deep doo-doo on this and it was getting deeper. St. Simon was not a person to play with. We had no idea how deep things had become until we got back to my store.

No sooner did I unlock the door and walk inside than two detectives from the city police came in to talk to us. They gave their names as Detectives Mallory and Johnson. They showed me their ID so quickly I barely got a good look. I thought it might be impolite for me to ask to see their ID more closely just then, so that I could actually make out the photos, and where their ID was actually from. I mean, for all I knew they could have been driver's licenses, or even fancy library cards, though I thought it was not the time to press the issue with them. They looked hard and rough. These were not the type you wanted to ever talk to, much less question. I realized they must have been in a car parked across the street, waiting for us to return to the store. They seemed anxious, impatient, while Juan and I were reluctant, cautious.

Mallory was a tall Irish-looking guy with a bad blond hairpiece, and Johnson a heavy-set black man with a pockmarked face and a cotton-top for hair. They wore rumpled suits, and looked tired and as worn out as their clothing, but they appeared to be the kind of guys you did not cross lightly. They seemed to have no sense of humor or patience at all. They were grim. Cold. They looked angry, even.

Juan gave me the watch-out-with-these-guys warning look. He did not have to do so.

After the introductions were gone through, we got down to business. Juan and I sat behind the counter in the back of my store and the two detectives stood in front of the counter, looking at all the old out-of-print and collectable books I had in the display case. Some of my most rare and expensive items were in there, and the cops looked them over, marveling and commenting on some of the prices.

'People really pay these prices for all these old books?' Mallory asked me, seemingly amazed. Was he just making small talk to set me at ease, or was he really interested? I wondered.

'Some do,' I stated flatly.

'Yeah, I remember that one. I had that book when I was a kid. Actually it was my father's book and he gave it to me when I was just a boy,' Mallory announced, pointing to a Tom Corbett Space Cadet hardcover in jacket. It had a stunning Lou Glanzman space painting on the dust jacket. Not my most expensive item by any means, but a lovely and eye-catching volume for sure. A very nice condition copy of a classic 1950s science fiction adventure novel nonetheless.

'It's one of a series of eight hardcover novels by Carey Rockwell published by Grossett & Dunlap in the 1950s. But you didn't come here to talk about old books, did you, Detective Mallory?' I stated flatly.

Juan smiled; he knew the drill. Small talk first to ease the marks, then get to the serious business with questions that threw them off their game.

'No, Mr. Jones,' Johnson, his partner, spoke up now. He pointed to the plywood that covered one of my broken front windows. 'We see you had some trouble recently.'

'Neighborhood kids. No big deal,' I stated, shrugging it off as best I could, even though it still rankled me. What was this neighborhood coming to?

'Sure,' Detective Johnson said, not believing me for a moment. 'Look, we need to know what you know about the death of Joseph Adler.'

'You mean the *murder* of Joseph Adler?' Juan corrected the detective.

'Yeah, well, you see, that's also part of why we're here,' Mallory continued testily. 'There seems to be some confusion on that score, and there shouldn't be.'

'Joseph Adler was murdered, Detective,' I stated firmly, throwing it out there to see their reaction.

Mallory looked at me hard. 'No, Mr. Jones, he wasn't. You're wrong. It was an OD. Overdose. Heroin. So I wouldn't be going around bothering people with questions and starting trouble over something you have no business being involved in.'

'Starting trouble!' Juan barked in anger.

'Cool down, boy!' Mallory ordered.

'Easy now, Juan, please,' I offered in an effort to sooth my young and impulsive friend. Then I looked over at the cops. 'Look, detectives, we already spoke to Dr. Williams at the ME's office. He assured us the death of Adler will be determined to be murder once the final autopsy report is issued.'

'Oh, he did, did he?' Johnson said sharply, shaking his head dubiously. I began to get a bad feeling about this now.

'Look, Mr. Jones — and you also, Mr. Marcano,' Mallory began firmly, 'we just came from Dr. Williams. I have a copy of the medical examiner's report right here, completed by Dr. Towbridge himself, who actually performed the autopsy. Your friend Williams was not the ME on this case, just another butinsky — like you two. Read it for yourself. The determination is death from an accidental overdose of heroin. There was no murder committed, and you two have no cause nor jurisdiction to investigate his death *in any way, shape, manner or form*. You're not even licensed investigators, you're just meddling busybodies with too much time on your hands. You need to stop churning up trouble and bothering people with this, or you could find yourself in a world of hurt.'

'Let me see that report,' I demanded.

Mallory shrugged and handed it over to me.

I read it, as did Juan, and the two of us were utterly stunned. 'This can't be right,' I stammered in surprise.

'It is,' Mallory stated simply, a sharp snarl to his lips.

'Overdose?' Juan asked. 'I can't believe it. It doesn't make any sense.'

'I'm going to call Dr. Williams and get this straightened out right now,' I said.

Mallory shrugged. He and his partner

waited patiently while I dialed the number. I got through right away.

'Dr. Williams?' I asked, using my professional voice, and not wanting to call him by his first name and let on to the detectives the fact that we were old friends.

'Yes, Thomas,' I heard Williams reply softly. 'I expected your call.'

'Then it's true, what the cops are showing me in the autopsy report from Dr. Towbridge? It says Joseph Adler's death was due to an accidental OD and not murder,' I said, dumbfounded. He had told me the exact opposite only that very morning. What the hell had changed since then and now — and why?

'Yes, Thomas. I'm sorry. There were complications; other items to consider. Significantly, it seems there were complications in the toxicology report; and since I had not performed the autopsy, I must yield to the findings of Dr. Towbridge.'

'I thought you were going to call me?' I stammered, trying not to let my anger boil over into foul language and a heated attack. 'I thought you were *sure* it was murder? You said you were going to dispute the findings and issue your own counter-report? What the hell happened?'

'I'm sorry, Thomas, really I am,' Williams said softly. I could hear the nervousness and guilt in his voice. 'There's really nothing else I can do about this now. I have to think of my status here, my pension. I have two years to go before I retire. I can't rock the boat now. I'm sure you understand how it is. I have to yield to Dr. Towbridge's findings.'

It was most unlike Ted. I could see he was under pressure. So were Juan and I. 'Sorry doesn't cut it, Ted. You lied to me! *Or someone got to you!*'

'That's uncalled for, Thomas, even from you!'

'Yeah, uncalled for! Who got to you, Ted? These two cops?'

'Hey!' Mallory barked in anger, his face beet red.

I looked at him sharply, then the phone went dead. Dr. Williams had bailed on me; he had hung up the line. I looked at Juan, whose face was frozen in anger as well. I sighed and put down my phone.

Slowly. Thoughtfully. It was as if I was in a trance. I didn't know what to do any longer.

'So, you clear on this now, gentlemen?' Mallory asked, looking over at Juan and me intently. 'It's over! Done! We're going now. We're done here, and you're done with this case. You keep prying where you're not supposed to and we'll bring you in for obstruction, harassment . . . we'll figure something. Get my drift, Professor? You're a smart fellow. Got brains. Back off, it'll be a lot better for you and the kid that way. Just take this as a friendly warning, all right?'

Mallory and Johnson turned around and walked towards the door to leave. Mallory noted my window with the plywood covering the broken glass. 'See what happens when you get involved with things you shouldn't get involved with? By the way, this is a nice bookstore you got here. You should stick to books and leave deaths and such to the professionals.'

Juan and I watched them leave. We were holding our breaths with an intense anger we'd never felt before.

'Bastards!' Juan growled under his breath.

'Yeah, real bastards!' I said grimly. 'I wonder what's going on with the murder of Joseph Adler?'

'*Viejo*, whatever it might be, we seem to have stirred up a real hornets' nest.'

'You ain't kidding, kid.'

'Don't call me kid, *Viejo*.'

'Then don't call me *Viejo*, kid.'

11

We Find the Evidence

'Well, what now, *Viejo*?'

I looked at Juan with growing annoyance, then just gave up and shook my head. We had more serious things to consider now, most notably what we were going to do about Joseph Adler's murder. Should we step out of it like the cops had told us? Or ignore them and go full steam ahead, with all that could mean? I know Juan was all for the latter. At the moment I was unsure of exactly how I felt. Everything seemed so complex and confusing. We needed some solid leads. And then there was St. Simon. I didn't even want to think about him.

'So what do you think?' Juan asked me, sitting on the stool behind the back counter, with my old cash register in front of him. My store was open for business, but there were no customers. Juan and I were alone, and *we felt* very alone.

'I don't know. Adler was definitely murdered, but those two cops . . . they give me the creeps. The autopsy report and cause of death make it all look legit.'

'Look legit?' Juan offered with a smirk. 'Yeah, well . . . someone got to someone.'

'You think so?' I asked, and I had to admit I had the same uneasy feeling.

'Bought off cops?' Juan asked me, nodding, apparently pretty sure of the fact, and I could see he didn't like the two cops one bit either.

I sighed. 'I'm not sure about them. They may just be taking the course of least resistance. They see Adler as just another dead junkie, and no one cares about a junkie murder. They want it out of the way. Case closed.'

'People care, *Viejo*. You and I care. That old couple cares,' Juan reminded me. 'Even Andrea Tatos cares.'

'Yes, that's true, but no one else does. Not those cops. No one that really matters. And I don't like how those cops seem much too interested in us.'

Juan nodded sadly, acknowledging that

truth. Then, changing the subject, he added, 'So what about Charles St. Simon?'

'Now he's a different kettle of fish altogether. Did you see his face when we mentioned the tin dispatch box? I agree with you now that he was scared, Juan. A big-time criminal like him, and he was really scared.'

'Yeah. You think there's gold in that box, or cash? Maybe diamonds or jewelry? I mean, there's gotta be something very valuable in there . . . Maybe some kind of important papers, or some sex photos maybe? You know, stuff like that like for blackmail?'

'I don't know; we're just guessing. St. Simon's got all the money he needs, and his type are always greedy for more. But I didn't see greed in his face. I saw fear. That means whatever's in that box has to be something of a personal nature. Something he fears getting out that could be a danger to him, or hurt him,' I said thoughtfully.

'*Viejo*, you're figuring it out just like Sherlock Holmes would do. I'm very impressed with you.'

'Why, thank you, Juan. That's very nice of you to say, though not at all accurate.'

'That's true. After all, *I'm* Sherlock. You're supposed to be Watson, remember?' Juan countered with his sly smile. 'I think this Joseph Adler was playing a very dangerous game.'

'Okay, Sherlock, so what's our next move?'

Juan studied me inquiringly. 'So the two detectives didn't discourage you any?'

'A bit. I have to admit they gave me food for thought, but they only made me realize how much more we have to find out in this case. It's murder. We have to clear it up. I'm more determined than ever to do that,' I stated firmly.

'Bravo, Watson!' Juan shouted. 'I knew I could count on you!'

'Hah!' I blurted, feigning annoyance. 'Why are you always passing me off as Watson and yourself off as Sherlock?'

'Why? Well, isn't it obvious?'

'No, not really,' I shot back, rather piqued.

'Well, it's elementary, Professor,' Juan

said, giving me his winning smile. 'I will do so just as Holmes would to Watson. Is that not correct? It is so elementary because *I am the one who knows what our next step must be.*'

I looked at him sharply, curious. 'And prey tell, what would that be, Mr. Sherlock?' I said sarcastically.

'The next step is finding that tin dispatch box, and I have a hunch where it might just be hidden.'

I looked at my young partner in a new light. 'Really?'

'Yes, really.'

'Not kidding with me, are you?'

'I certainly am not!' Juan shot back sharply, showing me he was a bit upset at my lack of faith in his words.

'Well, don't keep it a secret. What have you found out?'

'It is what I've *deduced*. Deduction is the key to any proper investigation. Or so Sherlock Holmes told us in the stories.'

'Yes?'

'So, let's go. We have to take a ride back to the Adler home,' Juan told me carefully as he put on his coat and walked out from behind the counter of my store. 'And *Viejo*, do you happen to have a shovel handy?'

I did. It was in the back room of my store, and I put it in the trunk of my old Chevy Aveo. Then I locked up my store and we got in the car and drove off to the Adler home once again.

* * *

We got there in no time. We were invited in by the elderly grandparents of Joseph Adler, his only living relatives, and they allowed us into the back yard seemingly not very concerned what we were going to do there. I carried the shovel.

'Why are we here?' I asked full of curiosity.

'What do you think?'

'I don't know. I guess you think Adler buried the box out here? Somewhere here in the back yard?'

'It's as good a place as any. The box was not anywhere in the house; I looked all over. I don't think Adler had any time to hide it anywhere else where I couldn't find it. That would take too much time, be too involved. He had to do it fast, so he had to find a good place for it — a place that no one would figure, but one that he could get to easily. Adler didn't take it with him when he left — no one saw it. It wasn't found on his body. He wanted that box out of the house, but he'd want it nearby where he could get at it quickly if he needed to. He might just have buried it out here in the back yard,' Juan stated very succinctly, full of confidence.

I marveled at his thought processes. 'You really did read all those Sherlock Holmes stories and actually learned something from them, didn't you?'

'I took them rather seriously, *Viejo*,' Juan admitted dryly.

I handed him the shovel. 'Well, since you're so young and I'm such an old *Viejo*, you can be the one to do the digging.'

Juan frowned but he took the shovel, adding, ' 'Old *Viejo*' is a double negative.'

'Yeah, and shoveling is something for young men to do, not older men.'

'*Old* men, *Viejo*.' Juan took the shovel

and led me around the house into the back yard.

The yard was rather large, with many small trees, which meant a lot of leaves on the ground this time of year. I figured we'd be there a while. It didn't look like there was anything there, at least at first glance. Nothing was obvious to me at all, but I knew that didn't necessarily mean anything. What we were looking for would certainly be hidden and not easy to find.

'I don't see signs of any recent digging out here,' I mentioned, suddenly feeling a bit of disappointment. My hopes were dashed. The yard looked to be undisturbed for a long while.

Juan did not relent. He carried the shovel over his shoulder, walking around the yard in concentric circles from the bordering fence towards the center garden table and chairs. 'I learned this, I think, from *The Musgrave Ritual*.'

'You did?' I asked in awe.

'I think it was from that story. All these leaves from the trees are obscuring the dig spot, if it's here. You'll have to brush them all away.'

'Me? Why me?' Not that I cared about it all that much, but I chafed at his seeming authority to order me around so brazenly.

'I'm doing the shoveling, *Jefe. Comprende*?'

I nodded. It was only fair. So I began gathering the leaves with a garden rake I found leaning up against the back fence. 'By the way, do we know how big this tin dispatch box is?'

'Yes. The grandfather said it was rather small. I would say four inches high, twelve inches long and eight inches deep, or thereabouts. I believe it may, in fact, be Watson's tin dispatch box, the very box he mentions in the Sherlock Holmes stories.'

Watson's 'travel-worn and battered tin dispatch box', as it is described exactly in the original Doyle stories, was said to reside somewhere in the vaults of the bank Cox & Co., at Charring Cross. The box had the words 'John H. Watson, M.D., Late Indian Army' painted upon the lid. It was said to be crammed with records of Holmes cases. Even more interesting, there were over 100 cases Watson referred to in the original stories that he chose for one reason or other *not* to write about. If any of those stories were in that box . . . Well, I shook with delight and sheer anticipation at the very thought. Could Juan actually find that box? Did it exist? And if we found it, what would we find within it?

I said softly, 'Now that would be a real discovery!'

'Yeah, but it depends on what's in it, if anything.'

'Yes, that's true.' My mood was now more grounded as my hopes of what might lay within that box became more realistic. What would the chances be that we would find Watson's old story notes? Pretty dire, I figured. It would be a miracle if we even found the box. Or any box, whether or not it had once belonged to Watson at all. Even that might not be true; it might just be one big hoax, even if we did find it. Some kind of counterfeit or forgery. It gave me grim food for thought.

I watched with interest as Juan examined the ground, moving a few leaves I had missed in my raking duties; but he did so carefully so as not to disturb the dirt underneath. It didn't appear that there was any place in the yard where Joseph Adler may have recently dug a hole. I was stymied, and I could see that Juan was growing impatient.

'It doesn't look good,' I said sadly.

'It's not supposed to be easy, *Viejo*. Don't give up just yet.'

I nodded, continuing my visual examination of the yard once again. I didn't know exactly what I was looking for. There wasn't much there to hide even a small tin box: a few trees, an old wooden barbecue table and some lawn chairs, a small garden with rather unhealthy flowers and weeds, and a coffin-sized outdoor storage box. We'd already checked the barbecue and storage box carefully. The latter was full of cushions for the garden chairs and a hose used to water the lawn — a lawn that looked like it had not been watered since last year.

'Nothing?' I asked, somewhat dejected.

'Not yet,' Juan answered, but I could see he was thinking fast. He went over to the garden again, examining it more closely. There were various plants growing there sparingly: some vegetables and flowers and a lot of weeds, none of which seemed to be very healthy, and none of which obstructed our view of the ground. He pulled out a few, shook his head, and stood back up looking intently at the garden.

'You think it could be buried in the garden?' I asked, wondering if the plants were doing so poorly because of neglect, or some other reason. Maybe a tin box buried underneath would affect their health? I wondered about that, and mentioned it to my young companion.

Juan just ignored me, deeply focused on something. Then he slowly walked away from me and over to the outdoor storage box. He opened the lid and looked inside.

'We already checked in there,' I reminded him.

'Yes, but I need you to help me move this. We checked inside, *Viejo*, but we didn't check *underneath*.'

I smiled, walked over to him, and together we moved the coffin-sized plastic storage box. It wasn't that heavy, even with the stuff inside it. I doubt Juan really needed my help to move it, but I was heartened that he had wanted to include me in his search, for it was what we saw underneath that really set my heart racing.

My eyes widened and I shouted, 'Newly dug ground!'

'Yes, just as I surmised,' Juan announced confidently.

Then my young partner took his shovel and began digging. I watched him in rapt fascination. Could this be it? I wondered what we would find buried there, if anything. I admit that I was transfixed watching Juan shovel out the dirt, creating a small hole. Finally he put the shovel down after I heard the sound — he had hit a solid metallic-sounding object.

Juan got down on his hands and knees and with his fingers carefully dug around the area, moving more dirt away. I got down and helped him. The two of us were now working frantically, ecstatic with wonder and anticipation, scraping away dirt from the hole. We were like children on a treasure hunt. It was exciting, fascinating, wonderful. We made the hole wider, deeper; and then suddenly something became visible and my friend pulled up a small metal box. He held it up triumphantly for me to gaze upon in wonder.

'I think we hit pay dirt, *Viejo*!' Juan shouted in victory.

I shouted now too, for when he held out the box to me I noticed the writing upon the lid and knew that what we had discovered was the Holy Grail of Holmes relics. I gasped in awe. Stunned. Overjoyed.

'Juan, that has to be it — Dr. John H. Watson's battered tin dispatch box. It really is Watson's box!' I shivered with joy.

'Yes, *Viejo*. We've made a historic find. See his name on it right here,' Juan said proudly, brushing off some of the remaining dirt from the box. 'This box proves that Watson was real! And if Watson was real, then Sherlock Holmes *must* be real too! I wonder what we'll find inside this box.'

'Come on, let's open it now!' I shouted, full of unbridled enthusiasm.

'All right,' Juan said, carrying the box and setting it down on the top of the garden table. Then he looked at me seriously. 'Now we find out the truth, Professor. Who knows what sacred documents might be inside?'

'In the stories, Watson wrote how he sealed his notes on many of the unwritten Holmes stories in his old battered tin dispatch box,' I babbled in excitement, my eyes staring at the box as if it were the Rosetta Stone or some other such sacred relic. My mind was reeling at just what might be inside that incredible box, and I fairly stammered, 'Untold tales, Juan, perhaps even *The Story of the Giant Rat of Sumatra* — a tale stated by Holmes himself as one for which the world was not yet prepared! Do we dare hope . . . ?'

'Ready, *Viejo*?' Juan asked me now, set to carefully pry the lock with his pocket knife and pop open the lid.

I swallowed in nervous but joyous anticipation. Sherlock Holmes and Dr. Watson had been my heroes since my youth. I'd grown up on the stories; loved all the books by Doyle and even the later pastiches by other authors. I knew Juan felt the same about Holmes as I did. This would be the verification of the lifelong dream of any Sherlockian to prove that Holmes and Watson were, in fact, real persons who had once actually lived!

'Sure, Juan, let 'er rip!'

Juan gingerly jimmied the old lock with his knife. It was not difficult, and it was breached with a telltale snap. Then my young friend looked at me, smiled broadly, and slowly lifted the lid and opened the box as we both frantically looked within.

12

That Which Lay Within

Our awe turned to surprise and then . . . to utter disappointment. Then even more surprise, but this time it was quite different.

'What's this?' Juan asked, shaking his head in utter confusion.

'A gun! A gun? Why?' I muttered, then brightened. Could it be Watson's very own revolver? I looked at it closely. No, I saw soon enough that it couldn't be.

'It's a gun in a clear plastic Ziploc bag,' Juan said thoughtfully as he stared at it. As yet, neither of us had even touched it. 'It looks like a .32 Beretta.'

'That's certainly *not* Watson's gun,' I said, even more disappointed now. 'And it's in a plastic bag. That means it's something more recent.'

'Yeah.'

I looked at my young friend and said

softly, 'Your father was murdered with such a gun.'

'I know,' Juan stated in shock. This was the last thing either of us had ever expected to find in that old tin box.

'Look underneath it — there's a note,' I said, carefully taking out the gun still in the plastic Ziploc bag, and placing it on the table in front of us. My action revealed a white piece of paper left at the bottom of the box. There was nothing else inside. No Watson letters, no new Holmes stories or case notes, just this one lonely letter sitting there by itself and seemingly mocking us by its very presence. I saw that it was written on recently made white paper. My disappointment seemed complete.

I looked at Juan, then I carefully took out the letter from the bottom of the box. It was folded in half, and I unfolded it carefully. It was typed and signed at the bottom, and contained a short note, very much to the point. I read it out loud:

This is the .32 Beretta used by Charles St. Simon to murder Alberto Marcano.

The gun is registered to St. Simon and I was able to free it from his possession. He is a noted gun collector, and could not destroy such a prize piece, but it links him to the Marcano murder solidly. His fingerprints are on the weapon and a ballistics test will prove that the bullets that killed Marcano came from this gun. The evidence of this gun will convict Charles St. Simon and destroy his drug and criminal empire once and for all.

The letter was signed, 'Joseph Adler.'

I looked at Juan in astonishment. He had become suddenly silent, shocked obviously by what he had just heard, and tears were streaming down his face. Poor kid; I didn't know what to say. He took the letter out of my hands and read it again to himself, slowly, carefully.

'I'm sorry, Juan,' I said softly and rather lamely. There was not much else to say; nothing that could make him feel better or bring his father back. Juan stayed silent, apparently struggling to believe what he was reading, but then I saw the light of joy come across his face.

'My father, *Viejo* . . . He wasn't a perfect man, but which of us is? He didn't deserve to die, though. I miss him. He'll be avenged and his murderer brought to justice. Finally!'

I nodded in total agreement, then I reminded my young partner, 'But St. Simon specifically told us he had nothing to do with your father's death.'

Juan allowed a grim smile. 'St. Simon is a career criminal, *Viejo*. They always lie. It's what they do. Lies come as second nature to them. No, we have proof now of a murder he committed himself years ago with his own gun. This gun! That's explosive stuff, real evidence. This gun will put him away, maybe even get him the chair. That's why he wants it back so bad.'

'And Joseph Adler stole it. I wonder why,' I said, brimming over with questions.

'We'll never know, *Viejo*, not for sure; but I think I can make a good guess. I think he wanted to set things right. I think it was as Holmes once said about 'art in the blood' — well in this case, it was him being of the blood of Sherlock Holmes and Irene Adler. Eventually he'd do what his blood told him to do.'

I nodded, dubious, but accepting his words about young Adler. Juan was right, of course, about the main thing. We now had the murder weapon — necessary evidence — but what should we do with it? Pass it on to those two detectives, Mallory and Johnson? I didn't think so. I didn't trust them at all, nor did Juan. What about other detectives? Well, that was the problem, wasn't it? Who could we trust? Juan put the situation in perfect perspective.

'Now that we have the evidence, who can we give it to, to put St. Simon away for murder?' Juan asked me thoughtfully.

I shrugged in confusion. 'I honestly don't know who we can trust. If we give the gun to the wrong person, it may just disappear, or even end up back with St. Simon. We're in a real jam, Juan. St. Simon will be after us soon too for this gun, so we have to do something fast.'

Juan nodded and looked at me closely.

'We have to go higher up.'

'Higher up in the police department? See a captain? Go to the police commissioner? The mayor?' I suggested, a bit frantic. What to do, indeed!

'I think not,' Juan stated firmly. 'We have to go to the news media. They'd like a story like this, and they're the only ones we can really trust now.'

I nodded. It made sense, and I did not really trust the police, so I said, 'Okay, Juan, I'm with you on that, I guess. It sounds good, but which media? Local TV? The newspapers? One of the internet news sites?'

'All of them,' Juan said sharply. 'We'll set up a press conference with all the media and the D.A. Tell them all in advance what we have. They'll take the bait. Then we'll hand the gun over to the D.A. in a public meeting with the media there reporting it all as witnesses. Then that gun can't disappear. Then we can't be shot either.'

I nodded at my young partner. It seemed like he had come up with a good plan. I folded up the letter written by

Joseph Adler, another key piece of evidence, and placed it back in Watson's battered tin dispatch box, then placed the .32 Beretta, still in the plastic Ziploc bag, on top of the letter in the box just as we had found it. I closed the lid.

My eyes fixated upon the writing on the lid of the tin box once again, and the name written thereon: 'John H. Watson, M.D.' I sighed. We'd found the missing box, and we'd discovered evidence that not only solved Juan's father's murder of years before but would put behind bars one of the most dangerous criminals in the city. Yet I felt so full of despair, so unfulfilled. We'd not yet discovered who had murdered Joseph Adler — which had been our original case — and there was another nagging question still in the back of my mind. If this really was Watson's old dispatch box, where were his missing writings? The box was said to contain a rare accumulation of notes and stories from unpublished cases of Sherlock Holmes. Where were they? Had they ever existed at all? Had Joseph Adler hidden them? A page from Watson's diary, or some notebook, had been discovered inserted into that 'Author Copy' of *The Strand Magazine* Adler had sold me so many days ago. Where was the rest of that book now?

13

St. Simon's Demise?

I made a call to a former police detective I knew. We were good friends and went back a few years. I'd obtained for him a teaching position at my college and he turned out to be a natural — a great teacher with actual 'real world' experience in what he taught. It doesn't get any better than that for a teacher. That was my friend, Barry Zaruba. Barry still had contacts on the police force with the higher-ups, and more more importantly in the D.A.'s office. That's because District Attorney Herman Zaruba was Barry's younger brother. So with Barry's help, we set up a meeting with the media and D.A. Herman Zaruba. It was to be held at police headquarters.

When we got there, Barry did the introductions, and then D.A. Zaruba took charge. We could see that he didn't especially like the idea of having the media there taking photos and notes, recording everything, but that was the condition we placed on our turning in the evidence we had found. We were scared to hold on to that gun for too long, in any event; it could mean a death sentence for us just as well as it could for St. Simon. We were eager to get rid of it, but we knew we had to get it into the right hands. I had mentioned to my friend Barry about our meeting with Detectives Mallory and Johnson. I asked him his opinion of them — I knew I could trust what Barry told me.

'They're good cops; they have a high closure rate,' Barry told Juan and me, then shrugged. 'But they cut corners. Sometimes a lot. They could be on St. Simon's payroll, maybe. Some cops in this town are, I know that for sure. Some politicians too, or he wouldn't be able to operate the way he does, so openly.'

I wasn't encouraged by these dire words. Then I looked at my friend and asked, 'I hope you won't take this the wrong way, but what about you, Barry?'

Barry Zaruba just smiled at my words. A lesser man would have taken them as a rank insult and walked out or just slugged me, but Barry was a friend and a good guy. He wasn't hurt by my question. He knew Juan and I were strung out and scared by all that had happened, suspicious of everyone now, almost paranoid. And with good reason. We were in way over our heads and knew it.

'It's all right to ask. St. Simon wasn't a major shot-caller when I was on the job back then. He was on our radar though, and he was moving up, making inroads with the drug gangs on the East Side. However he was not the big man he is today. One of his rivals was — ' Barry looked carefully at my young friend, Juan — 'Alberto Marcano.'

I looked at Juan and saw him nod slowly.

Barry continued, 'Anyway, I retired shortly after the Marcano murder. I didn't like the stink of it. I couldn't find any evidence to get St. Simon — or anyone else, for that matter — on it, but I was sure one of the rival drug dealers back then was involved. I wanted to dig deeper into St. Simon, but the bosses pulled me off the case. They said they couldn't spare men and resources on another dead drug dealer — they were popping up all over the city back then, if you remember. Drive-bys and revenge drug murders. It was real war back then on the streets. To this day, I think it was wrong to let it slip between the cracks. After that, well . . . being a cop just didn't have the same juice for me. I met you soon after and you got me the teaching gig at the college — for which I am eternally grateful, by the way. A much better environment, and the only blood spilled is from the occasional paper cut.'

I smiled and gave Barry a warm pat upon the shoulder, glad that he was not upset by my questioning, and gladder still that he was on our side. He was a good friend, and one of the good guys in my book. I noticed Juan standing nearby, silent and grim, probably thinking of his murdered father and the fact that even though he had been a drug dealer, his father's murder still cried out for justice.

At least with Juan it still did.

I knew that the murder of his father years ago had destroyed Juan's family and his happy life as a kid, setting him upon a path of self-destruction that only the gift of that Sherlock Holmes book to him by me had affected positively. I didn't know what to say about it all.

Juan said it all: '*Viejo*, you were there back then and you gave me that Sherlock Holmes book to read. It changed my life at a time when it was going all to hell. You and Sherlock Holmes, I thank you both . . . Now let's get down to present business, eh? We have a lot of work to do. We have the media here now setting up, and your friend Barry and D.A. Zaruba are waiting.'

'So where is this evidence you say will convict Charles St. Simon of the Alberto Marcano murder?' D.A. Zaruba asked us, growing impatient, looking over at the media people cautiously. There were quite a few of them setting up camera and microphones, taking out pens and note-pads, getting ready. You could see that as a politician he was wondering how to spin this to his advantage and get more votes. The elections were coming up, after all. I looked at him sternly. What a guy. Politicians!

The media people took their photos and wrote down their notes, asking us all our names, our titles, the proper spellings of our names — and probably getting most of it wrong. They ran their video cameras and tape recorders, and the hot lights shone upon us all. It began to get a bit uncomfortable. I grew nervous, but we ploughed ahead with the plan.

Juan got everyone's attention. 'The reason we are all here today is for this!' Then he pulled out the small tin dispatch box from a sack, opened the lid and placed the .32 Beretta — still sealed in the clear plastic Ziploc bag that Joseph Adler had originally placed it in — upon the table before us. The gun sat there like a mystical talisman. What did it mean? He also handed the D.A. Joseph Adler's letter. Then he closed the box and quickly replaced it back into the sack. We had agreed beforehand that it might be a good idea not to let the media know about the

Watson connection just yet — or for them to see Watson's name upon the box lid. It would have just complicated things needlessly.

Cameras clicked and eyes stared as Juan continued in a tense but powerful voice, 'This is the gun that was used to murder my father, Alberto Marcano. It's owned and registered to Charles St. Simon, with his fingerprints upon it, and ballistics will match the bullets that killed my father as being fired from this gun. His gun.'

There was stunned silence, then the media hounds almost as one began shouting out questions and clicking more photos.

Barry Zaruba, acting for his brother, got everyone to quiet down a bit so we could proceed.

'If what you say is true . . . ' D.A. Zaruba began. He was standing in front of us all quite brazenly, mostly for the media impact I suspect, and he got everyone's attention. They were busy snapping all kinds of photos and video, and had taken down our words with frenzied pens and high-held cell-phone cameras, now that the D.A. had begun the official spiel, ' . . . then I'll instruct Police Commissioner Rogers to have Mr. St. Simon brought in for questioning on this matter immediately, pursuant to an arrest, pending the lab report of course. Clarissa, will you please step forward?'

An older, serious-looking, rail-thin woman dressed in a white lab coat suddenly materialized from behind the large group of men surrounding the D.A. Zaruba continued, 'This is Clarissa MacDougal, the head of our crime lab and forensics department. She'll do a complete run-up on this weapon and issue a detailed report to me. If the ballistics and fingerprints match, then an arrest warrant will be issued for Mr. St. Simon for murder.'

I nodded. That sounded good. We seemed to be making progress now. More cameras clicked. I looked over at Juan, and he nodded back to me with a slight smile upon his face. It appeared that there was finally justice now for his murdered father. That was good. Now, I thought, what about Joseph Adler?

'It's gratifying that two such public-minded citizens as Professor Thomas Jones and Mr. Juan Marcano have come forward with this evidence to enable us to solve this longstanding murder case. While the case had gone cold, I can assure you all that it was never closed by this police department, or my office. I know that Mr. Marcano must find it especially gratifying to have a suspect in the murder of his father finally brought to justice after all these years, but we must remember that Mr. St. Simon is also innocent until proven guilty. We'll have to see what the evidence shows us; and if it goes there, then it'll be up to a jury to decide. I'm sorry for your loss, Mr. Marcano, but I assure you we'll do all we can to prosecute the man responsible, so long as the evidence you've presented us with today proves to be true. Justice will be served in this community,' the D.A. stated most seriously, like it was part of his reelection speech — which it may very well have been.

Barry Zaruba nudged me in the side.

'My brother just can't resist the cameras and the political spiel, but I'm sure he'll get to the bottom of this, Prof. The gun — your evidence — is in good hands now.'

'I hope so, Barry,' I told him, looking over at the D.A., who was basking in the glow from the photographers, as Ms. MacDougal carefully collected the gun and letter evidence. I looked to Juan and expected to see at least some measure of joy or relief upon his face, but instead I saw neither.

'I have one more question I'd like to ask you, D.A. Zaruba,' Juan Marcano said in a determined tone.

The cameras turned to Juan and clicked upon him now, the reporters turning to the young man whose father's murder might have been finally solved after all these years. 'Sir, we still need to know who murdered Joseph Adler. It was evidence that we originally discovered in trying to find his killer that led to my father's murderer being found out. But what about Mr. Adler? Where is his justice? I don't want him to be forgotten.'

‘He won’t be forgotten, I assure you,’ D.A. Zaruda said, looking concerned at the way this might now be going. Would it spiral out of control? Was Juan a loose cannon?

‘We’re working on that, son,’ Police Commissioner Rogers said, stepping forward to take the flack before the D.A. could speak any further. ‘We’re aware of the case. Joseph Adler was a troubled youth and a known drug user, and a distributor too. He was the victim of a heroin overdose, as far as we know. That’s what the autopsy has determined.’

‘That’s not true! Joseph Adler was murdered!’ Juan barked loudly.

The media frenzy hit full throttle then. Cameras shot more photos, quotes were furiously scribbled onto pads, video was rolling that would be shown on the evening TV news. More questions were shouted and ignored. I was beginning to wonder if this presser had been such a good idea.

It rankled me to hear Rogers’s explanation of Adler’s death, so I decided to add my own measure of gasoline to the fire. I said, 'It seems to me there's some sort of cover-up going on regarding the murder of Joseph Adler. It wasn't an accident. He *was* murdered!'

The words 'cover-up' got everyone's attention, and the members of the media seemed to ooze with hyperactivity at my use of that combustible phrase. I had said my words loudly, to allow them to be heard and to sink in, and I saw Juan nod to me approvingly. He was apparently happy that his cranky old man-partner had spoken his mind and got everyone's attention.

I continued firmly, 'Joseph Adler was given a hot shot of heroin; he was not a heroin addict. He'd been off the drug and clean for two years. He hated heroin and stayed clean. He was obviously murdered because of the evidence he possessed on the Marcano murder, which we've now turned over to the D.A. and the police today. I have to ask you here and now, Commissioner Rogers, an important question that could shed light upon his murder. Was Joseph Adler a police informant?'

My question had definitely added more fuel to the media fire, and they chomped at the bit for answers, peppering the commish and D.A. with many questions. Rogers looked extremely uncomfortable. He was about to attempt an answer when D.A. Zaruba whispered in his ear. Rogers nodded, apparently much relieved.

Then the D.A. suddenly faced the media and stated simply and dead-pan in his best bureaucratic legalese, 'Ladies and gentlemen, this has been a most productive meeting. We may have solved a longstanding murder case, and if the evidence proves true it will bring a murderer to justice. At this time, we'll hold off on any further questions until an official report has been issued. That will be all, ladies and gentlemen. Thank you all for coming — and once again, thank you Professor Jones and Mr. Marcano for bringing this evidence to our attention. That will be all, ladies and gentlemen, for now. Have a good day.'

Juan and I watched in open-mouthed surprise as D.A. Zaruba, Police Commissioner Rogers, Mayor Jameson and their entourage immediately left the meeting room. They were ushered away and gone with expert and time-worn precision. Barry Zaruba stayed behind with us. The media took more video and notes and then focused upon us, since they knew the pols were now gone and effectively unapproachable.

I swallowed hard, looking at all the media people and wondering what I would say or even if I *should* say anything more to them. Hadn't we said enough already? However, Juan had no problems in that area, as I would immediately find out.

Juan suddenly got everyone's attention and repeated my statement of moments before, saying that Joseph Adler had been murdered, that he was not a heroin addict, and that he had in fact been a police informant and had been murdered because of the evidence he had discovered. Juan was going great guns, then added, 'I'm also certain that it was Charles St. Simon, or one of his men acting under his orders, who gave Joseph Adler the hot shot that killed him.

Charles St. Simon is behind that murder as well!'

Well, pandemonium broke out among the press at that news. Having evidence was one thing the press could understand and accept, but more accusations . . . and unproven ones at that . . . I sighed and looked over at Juan, then at all the press people. They were on the hunt and had taken the scent. It seemed the only thing they liked better than the solving of an old crime was new charges being brought on a more recent murder. They pummeled us with a barrage of questions. We did what we could to answer them; but when they asked us what evidence we had for this new accusation, Juan and I realized we had gone too far. We had none. Just accusations, and some hunches that we thought fit the crime.

'How can you accuse Mr. St. Simon without any evidence? Is this just open season on him? Is it because he's a black man?' one woman asked, trying to get a bite from us.

'That's ridiculous!' I stammered, in what I know was most likely a futile defense. I swallowed hard, not liking at all where this questioning seemed to be going. I looked at Juan and he shook his head sadly at me. I guess when you play the accusation card, it can come back to bite you unless you can back it up. As yet, we had nothing on Adler's murder, and the media sensed it and pounced.

'The autopsy says Adler died of an OD. What evidence do you have to dispute that? Are you a medical doctor?' one man demanded, holding a mike in my face. I could not reply, however, because we had no evidence. I could have told him what we thought, guessed, believed, but we were in enough trouble already, so I kept mum.

'Isn't it irresponsible for you two to make these further charges against Mr. St. Simon without proper evidence?' a young TV anchorwoman now made her own charge against us. 'I mean, he hasn't even been formally charged with the first crime yet. Suppose your evidence doesn't pan out?'

'Don't you think it's odd that the D.A. is familiar with the autopsy report of a druggie who just OD'ed?' I said. 'The evidence will point out — '

'So you say,' the woman responded. 'Where's the proof?'

I sighed, and felt Barry Zaruba at my side. He could see the way the wind was blowing and shouted to the media, 'Evidence will be forthcoming, ladies and gentlemen. But for now, this press conference is over.'

Then Barry whisked Juan and me out of the room and down the hall before the news people knew what was happening. They followed us ravenously, catching up and bombarding us with more questions — and in some cases even rather nasty accusations. We ran to the elevator. Thankfully the door opened; Barry shoved Juan and me inside as he got in, and hit the button for the basement garage where my car was parked. We got down there just before the media did, jumped into my old Chevy Aveo, and got the hell out of there pronto.

14

A New Plan is Needed

Juan and I were back at my bookshop, talking over the events of the day. Barry Zaruda had gone on home but promised to keep an ear peeled to what his brother, the D.A., was doing on the case. Any action and we'd know it soon enough.

'A busy day, *Viejo*,' Juan said with an ironic laugh.

'I'll say. Those media people . . . they're like sharks! Here, have some more fries.'

We were eating some take-out hamburgers and fries and drinking root beer soda on the back counter of my store, using it as a makeshift table. We ate fast, sitting comfortably upon the stools I had behind the counter.

'Yes they are. That's their way.' Juan grinned, wolfing down his food.

I nodded, then shook it all off. 'But at least you must feel good that we found the evidence. And once it's been proven valid — and it surely will — your father's murderer will be brought to justice. Finally, St. Simon will be in prison where he belongs.'

'Yes, but what about the person who murdered Joseph Adler, *Jefe*?'

I nodded and took another bite of my burger. We still had some loose ends to clear up. 'Juan, I think you and I know that Adler had to be a police informant who worked in St. Simon's organization. Adler found the gun in St. Simon's house. Maybe he knew where it was stored, stole it, and then St. Simon murdered him for taking it.'

'Yes — so what?'

'Well, we've already got St. Simon for the murder of your father. He'll go away for a long time for that — or maybe even get the death penalty. Right now it might be a moot point whether he also gets the blame for Joseph Adler's murder. He's finished.'

Juan didn't like what I was saying, but he nodded. 'I guess you're right, *Jefe*.'

I hated it when he agreed with me,

especially now. It made me feel guilty somehow, and I felt some further explanation was needed. 'We have no evidence, Juan. You saw the way the media came after us. Without evidence on the Adler murder, we have nothing on St. Simon for that.'

'I know. I just wish there was some way we could avenge Joseph Adler's murder, especially now, since what he did for my pops. Maybe we could get one of St. Simon's goons to talk?'

'I doubt it. I mean we could try, but I really doubt that very much, Juan,' I said, rather hopelessly on that score. I had to be realistic. No one would rat in that bunch, even I could see that. They were all hardened criminals — stone-cold killers. But I didn't want to pass on my negativity to my young partner just then. So I said, 'Cheer up, lad. We did good. The evidence you found buried in that yard solved the murder of your father. It's a wonderful accomplishment.'

'Yes, *Jefe*. I'm proud of that, and it's a relief after so many years. So much bad has happened in my life; now I'm glad that some good has finally come into it.'

I nodded, looking at Juan and seeing that young kid of years ago to whom I'd given that Sherlock Holmes book — a book that had probably saved his life.

Suddenly the sound of breaking glass at my front window got our attention. Something had been thrown through the remaining glass window at the front of my store. Not another brick! I thought.

No, it wasn't any brick or rock this time. The explosion was thunderous and devastating. It took out most of the front of my store in a massive flash. Juan and I were immediately hurled backwards, down behind the counter, and it was only that very action which had given us the cover that probably saved our lives. The heavy wooden counter blocked the worst of the explosion.

I was stunned, down on the floor, surrounded by shards of glass and papers. Some of them I recognized with terror as being pages from obliterated books — *my* books!

'*Viejo! Viejo*, are you okay?' I heard a voice shout at me through the smoke.

There was smoke everywhere now, and fire. Books were burning! Oh, my God! My store was on fire!

I felt two rugged hands grab me and forcefully lift me upwards to my feet. 'Come on, we have to get out of here. Now! Get up!'

'Juan?'

'Yes. Are you okay, *Viejo*? Any bleeding? Pain?'

'I don't think so. Just shocked, stunned, and a bad ringing in my ears.'

'Me too.'

'What happened?' I asked numbly.

'A bomb,' Juan said simply.

'My God! Are you injured, Juan?'

'No, *Jefe*,' he answered as he lifted me carefully to my feet and led me out of the back of what was left of my store. There was no door there any longer. I stopped in the doorway and took one last look back into what was left of my lovely little bookstore and began to cry. There was not much left at all: it was a smoky, burning mess, and papers and books were burning everywhere. My God, my books were burning! I had to save them! But

Juan seemed to read my thoughts and held me back, ordering me harshly, 'We have to get out of here. Now!'

I continued to cry as he led me out the back of my store into the alley that led to the front street. I thought of all the lost books, the burning books that were being destroyed. Priceless objects I had collected all my life. Valuable books I had lovingly collected for a lifetime. Important books! Soon they'd be all gone. The fire was getting worse. Smoke damage would be the least of it. The fire would burn most of what was in my store, I was sure; then it would all be gone.

Fire is not good for books.

I heard sirens now, coming closer fast. The police and firemen were on the way. All I could do was think that would mean tons of water used by the firemen to douse out the raging flames, and whatever books not ruined by the fire would surely be destroyed by the water.

Water is not good for books.

My store was a total loss, I realized as Juan led me through the alley and onto the front street and safety. At that moment I didn't even care.

'Come on,' Juan scolded me, 'you'll be all right. That was a bomb. Someone is after us, but no need to cry about it. Thankfully we're safe.'

I looked at my young friend harshly. 'I'm crying for the store, Juan. For all my books. They'll all be destroyed, ruined; nothing will be left. They were all like good friends to me. Now they're gone forever.'

'Oh,' he said softly, realizing my feelings and suddenly empathizing with them. 'I'm sorry about your store, *Jefe*. I'm sorry about all your books.'

I didn't say another word. I just sobbed, an emotional wreck, so sad, feeling sorry for myself I guess. My bookstore was all I had in the world. It was not only a hobby and a passion, it was my livelihood in my old age. There was no way I could replace these items. And insurance? I thought about that now, of course. Well, insurance for such items is a joke. Unaffordable. There was no hope to save or replace any of it.

I was devastated, but I was still alive,

and Juan and I were both unharmed, and that really was the important thing. Though honestly, just then, it didn't seem to be all that important to me with the loss of my store and all my books. I was still processing what had happened, still in shock and anger. That anger was growing like the ringing in my ears from the explosion. The major thing, of course, was that a murder attempt had been made upon our lives. Someone had bombed my store in order to kill us. Someone had to pay for that!

The cops came pretty quickly, uniformed police, asking what happened. They began moving the mob of curious people back from what was left of the store, some of whom I recognized as my customers. The cops spread out yellow crime-scene tape as a barrier. The firemen came next and set up water cannons. They had the fire out soon enough, but they'd totally drenched my store, which meant they had poured water over my entire inventory. Every book was now a soggy, wet, destroyed mess. I doubted I could salvage much of what was left, but at that moment I didn't even care. I wasn't capable of thinking clearly about it. I couldn't even look.

The firemen did their work and soon left. EMS had also arrived, but Juan and I were unharmed other than a few tiny glass cuts, nothing serious. We had been lucky. EMS put a few bandages on our cuts, and then they left too.

The detectives finally arrived. It was our old friends, Mallory and Johnson. They walked over to Juan and me briskly. We were seated together, huddled on a stoop a few stores down from where my store had once been. Juan held me tightly; I was still shaking with shock and anger.

'What the hell do you want?' Juan blurted at the detectives. They looked contrite, or tried to at least, giving us their best 'sorry for your loss' look.

'Any idea who would do this?' Mallory asked.

'Yeah, you and your partner!' Juan cried out in so much rage that I had to actually restrain him. 'Look at his store! Look at the old man! That store was his life! Someone tried to kill us with a bomb! What the hell you going to do about that?'

Johnson held out his hands in a defensive gesture. 'Look, I know you're upset — '

'Upset!' Juan shouted. People were looking over at us with concern and interest. 'Upset don't even come near what I feel now, man!'

'All right.' Johnson backed off, shaking his head as if this were all *our* fault. Maybe in his way of thinking, it was. Our fault for getting involved in things we should not have become involved in.

I looked up at the two detectives and saw that behind them reporters and TV crews were now coming onto the scene. I shook my head. 'Keep them away from us, please.'

Mallory saw the media hounds advancing, and called over a uniformed cop and told him to keep them all back behind the yellow crime-scene tape and away from us. Mallory came closer, then bent down to look into my face. 'I'm sorry. Really.'

'Yeah?' Juan blurted. It was obvious he didn't trust these guys at all. Neither did

I. 'You probably did it.'

Mallory's face grew red with anger, then embarrassment perhaps, his lips pursed tightly. Then he stated, 'I *am* sorry. We had nothing to do with this, nothing at all, I promise you.'

'Then who the hell did?' Juan demanded.

'That's what we want to find out. Will you help us?'

'Then why did you try so hard to push us off the case the other day?' I asked bluntly.

Mallory shook his head sadly, regretfully. 'Because this is just the kind of thing I was worried might happen, with you and the kid there getting involved over your head. Well, you were lucky — you found the gun that might put St. Simon away, and I'm proud of you both for that. But he's still out on the street. He's got lawyers. Good lawyers. Goons. Hired killers. He's after you both now. Finding that gun might have been the worst thing you could have done, safety-wise.'

'Can't you arrest him?' I almost pleaded.

'Not until the ballistics confirms his gun is the murder weapon. We don't have that report yet. Even then, even with that, there's a chance he'll get bail and be out free until his trial. We'll watch him, but that won't be good for you. Even if he's locked up, he can still order one of his men to — '

'Damn! But he's a kingpin drug dealer!' Juan growled impatiently.

'He's *assumed* to be behind drug distribution on the East Side, but he's never been convicted of anything major — and he's done a lot of good local community service work, positive stuff. He supports the PAL for Christ sakes,' Mallory stated, looking downward. Was it in shame?

I shook my head, fear and anger raging inside me. I had to calm myself or I'd bust a blood vessel; my head would explode with the feelings swirling within me. So with an effort I calmed down, and calmed Juan down. After all, we were still both alive and unharmed. That was a positive. I knew Juan was much more volatile than me. The bombing and this news canceled out any joy from our victory over St. Simon earlier that day.

'What now?' I asked the detectives.

'We take you two into protective custody,' Johnson said simply.

I shook my head no.

'I'm afraid there's no other way,' Johnson insisted. 'It's for your own safety.'

'I want to be a lot more proactive after this. We could try to get the goods on St. Simon,' I said angrily.

'And how do you propose to do that?' Johnson laughed, shaking his head at me in frustration. I wondered why he was so damn frustrated! Juan and I were the ones who had almost been killed. Then he added, 'What, an old man and a wet-behind-the-ears kid? Come on! You're a professor, or at least used to be one before you retired. You're smarter than that. You can't seriously think of going up against a guy like St. Simon and hope to win.'

'We can try!' Juan blurted defiantly.

'You're both nuts!' Johnson proclaimed, and turned away.

'Yeah, we're nuts,' I said, and left it at that.

Juan took me home to my place; it was only a few blocks away. We were able to get away from the media, slipping away in the darkness. On the way I noticed my Chevy Aveo had also been destroyed in the blast. I had parked my battered old Chevy in a space directly in the front of my store. I almost never got that prime parking spot, but this evening I had and considered myself lucky. Now my car was a total ruin too, gone along with my store.

My whole life was in ruins. I was broke, my business was destroyed, even my car was gone — but at least I was still alive and as yet unharmed. That was something. In fact, truth be told, after all we'd been through, that was the only important thing. However, I was struck by the oppressive thought that even that might not last that long the way things were going.

Juan helped me up the stairs and put me in my recliner, then went into the kitchen to boil some water for coffee. I sat alone in my small living room, sobbing deeply, and then suddenly a smile came to my face. I looked around my apartment, seeing it in a new way now. I was a book collector! I had a book collection right there in front of me. I looked at all the shelves stuffed with books. So many books! Great stuff! It was my private, personal collection, the better and more valuable items I didn't sell or keep in the store.

I looked at all the shelves stuffed with so many wonderful valuable books and suddenly I realized that my apartment was nothing but a bookstore with a bed and table in it — and a bookstore that had much better stock than my former store ever did. My sobbing stopped. I didn't feel sorry for myself any longer. I realized that I was back in business. I could open a new store and use my collection to stock it with. It could work. I smiled for the first time in hours.

Juan came into the room with two steaming cups of coffee. He handed me one cup, noticed me smiling, and I saw a look of concern cross his face. 'You look strange. You okay, *Jefe*?'

'Better. My store and all my books are gone, lost — but I have so many books here that I can start up another store, maybe even a better one. Maybe once all this mess is over, Juan.'

'Yes, that's the spirit. Like Holmes and Watson, we have our setbacks, but we never give up. Now drink your coffee while it's still hot.'

I nodded and took a sip. It was certainly hot, but I almost choked. 'Your coffee, it . . . sucks! What's this, instant?'

'Well thanks! Look, it's all I could find.'

'I don't ever drink instant. I just keep it for a lady friend when she comes over.'

'Ah, a lady friend! The secret life of *El Viejo*! Now it all comes out, I think,' Juan said, laughing with a mischievous leer.

'No sex, just a lot of talk,' I told him defiantly, but feeling vaguely sad about it all.

'Oh, you disappoint me.'

'I disappoint myself, Juan.'

He gave me a warm grin, put his coffee cup down, and looked at me carefully. 'You better now? You back with me?'

'Yes. I'm hurt, you know inside, by what happened. I'm angry. I want to get whoever did this, Juan.'

'Me too. It was most certainly done on the order of St. Simon — at least that's what I think.'

'You *think*?'

Juan shrugged. 'I think. I'm sure. Almost.'

I looked at him closely. *Almost* didn't quite cut it, but I knew what was really bothering him. 'You're thinking about those two detectives. You think they could have . . . ?'

'I don't know. At first I thought maybe, then yes for sure — they must be on St. Simon's payroll. But now I think not. They're overworked, underpaid, and much too grouchy — really miserable bastards. Cops on the take are different, more . . . secure, and they don't care about cases.'

'So you think they're honest cops?'

'I think so. It's possible. Look at their clothes — pure crap. Disheveled. I mean, even *you* wouldn't wear a suit like Mallory's.'

'Thanks, Juan.'

He laughed good-naturedly. 'No offense, *Viejo*; you just wear some funky old duds. Anyway, that proves they got no money too. No one's paying them big bucks, or at least they're not spending anything on good clothes, that's for sure. At least that's the way it looks to me now. I'll tell you something else. They seem to know the score about things. I think, in their own screwed-up cop way, they really were looking out for us.'

'Really? So what now?'

'We have to trap St. Simon,' Juan stated simply.

'Well that's nice. I'm glad to hear it's not going to be anything too difficult for us to do. Just how the heck do we accomplish that?' I asked him in a tone full of biting irony, looking at my young friend with utter defeat and curiosity. He'd read some Sherlock Holmes stories as I had. He loved the stories, even had learned from them; but we were not Sherlock Holmes, nor Dr. Watson. I told him, 'Look, Juan, we're exactly what that detective said — an old man and a wise-ass kid, and we're in way over our heads and going up against a criminal mastermind like St. Simon who has a large organization behind him. We're fools, and we're finished.'

'Well, Holmes and Watson went up against Moriarty, and he had a large organization behind him, and they brought him down.'

I had to laugh at that. 'Juan, that's fine,

but that's fiction, my boy. This is real life. Real life gets people killed. Buildings get bombed, blown up.'

'*Jefe*, I understand what you're saying; but who's to say now, with what we've discovered, that Sherlock Holmes and Dr. Watson weren't real people after all? We did find that tin dispatch box from Cox & Co. That's Watson's very own box, I'm sure of it. So if Holmes and Watson were real, then they *did* take down Moriarty and his entire organization. So who's to say we can't do the same thing with St. Simon?'

'I don't think so, Juan. Anyway, I'm not entirely convinced that just because Watson's name is on the lid, the box was his. I mean, someone could've put it there. It could be a fake, a forgery. Maybe Joseph Adler painted it there himself for some reason. There's that connection in his family background, which we know is true; but there was nothing in that box that leads to the real Holmes or Watson, just your father's murder. Come on, you're grasping at straws here.'

'No, *Jefe*. With all due respect, you're

not seeing all the straws. It's as Holmes and Watson would do. Remember the stories. Remember Holmes's methods,' Juan insisted. 'Holmes would say, you *look* but you do not *see*, Watson! I say, you read the books but you do not *feel* the words in your heart and your mind.'

'I resent that, Juan!'

'No, don't resent it, embrace it! There has to be a way to bring down St. Simon. And we can do it!'

'I don't know, Juan.'

'Well, I do. I also know that this Joseph Adler, Irene Adler's great-grandson, had something that ties him to Holmes. Don't forget that piece of paper from the notebook or diary. Is it still in your safe at the store?'

I was startled; I'd forgotten all about that. For a second I feared it was gone too, lost in the fire, along with that copy of *The Strand Magazine* Alder had sold me so many days ago that had begun this case. Then I remembered I'd placed both securely in my safe. 'It may have made it through the fire by being locked in the safe.'

'Good — I think so too. That's a clue we need — our clue to Holmes and Watson; and maybe it'll help us with our own Moriarty, Charles St. Simon. Then we can avenge your store — and Joseph Adler.'

'All right,' I said, confused but willing to go along with anything that moved us forward. 'I'm with you, Juan.'

'Good man! Now give me the combination to that safe. I'll go get the paper and the magazine and bring them back here for us to examine. It may give us a clue.'

I doubted that, but I gave Juan the combination, and he was gone and back in a flash with a small bundle.

15

The Strand Magazine and the Diary Page

Juan gave me the *Strand Magazine* and the page torn from what I hoped was Watson's secret diary or notebook, a book now apparently lost to the ages, but that had once existed as proved by this last remaining rare page ripped out from it.

'What do you notice about it?' Juan asked me as I looked over the old magazine again and the torn-out diary page.

I shrugged. 'A nicely presented copy of *The Strand Magazine* from July, 1891 containing the Holmes story *A Scandal in Bohemia*. A stamped inscription at the bottom of the cover says 'Author Copy,' and tucked inside the magazine is a page that appears to be torn from a diary or notebook.'

'Correct. Simple enough. Now what does the page say?'

I smiled; Juan was playing Holmes. Okay, I would bite — I could tamp down my pride and play Watson again. I looked over the page carefully. 'It's quality bond paper. The ragged edge tells me it was torn from a book, probably a diary or notebook, and done rather hastily. You can date this page by the webbing in the paper. It is old, easily from a hundred years ago.'

'Very good, Professor. Now channel your inner Watson!'

'Really, Juan!'

'Come on. What else? What about what's written there?'

I read the note to myself once again. 'The date of the entry is March 20, 1888. That is the probable date of the events in the story *A Scandal in Bohemia*.'

'Yes. Go on.'

'Well, the facts of the case are outlined as if Doyle himself wrote the story, but I don't think this page was written by Doyle at all. Then in the margin I see, hastily scrawled in a different ink and hand, the cryptic sentence, 'Holmes seems to think the Irene Adler affair the best to recount/rewrite from notes and then present draft to Doyle/see what he thinks/JW 25/2/90.' That's February 25, 1890.'

'So then what?' Juan asked curiously, prodding me.

'It does seem to give us confirmation of Watson's existence. I imagine then, by that inference, it also gives us confirmation of Holmes himself being an actual person.' I said this slowly, unable to keep a hint of awe from creeping into my voice.

'Now, Joseph Adler sold you this when he knew St. Simon's men were after him,' Juan stated, thinking the puzzle through piece by piece. 'I believe this issue of *The Strand* and the torn page were the original and only contents of the tin dispatch box.'

'Really?'

'Those two items and nothing more, *Viejo*.'

I nodded rather sadly. I accepted what he was saying, but I had expected — even hoped — for far more.

Juan continued, 'Adler switched them with the gun and his letter about St.

Simon. Then he buried the box in his grandparents' back yard under the storage bin. He sold you the old magazine with the torn diary page inside it, to keep it safe. It was his one link to his famous great grandparents — Irene Adler and Sherlock Holmes. He didn't want it lost and forgotten. So he sold it to you, knowing you were an antiquarian bookseller who greatly valued such items.'

'But if it's authentic, it's a priceless piece! Why did he only take two hundred dollars for it?' I asked, stunned.

'I thought about that, and it had me stumped at first. Then it came to me. Could you afford to pay the actual value for such an item, *Jefe*? Sotheby's would auction such a relic at a million dollars — maybe a million pounds. Come on, think about it. He sold it to you for safekeeping. He knew he was going to be murdered. He was one of St. Simon's drug dealers working on the West Side, and he stole the gun out of St. Simon's home, from the gun collection of his boss, when he was a guest — the height of disrespect. By some accounts Adler was an up-and-coming dealer in the organization. St. Simon allowed him in his home, so perhaps the drug kingpin liked and took a personal interest in Adler. But Adler led a double life; he was a police informant — or maybe not. He might have been working his own game, something that we haven't discovered yet. Remember, the police refuse to admit he was an informant or a C.I. at all. He's dead now, so there's no reason for them not to be forthcoming on this information, if it was true. Maybe Adler was a rogue agent of some kind, operating on his own.'

'Some kind of vigilante?' I asked curiously.

'You might've hit upon it, *Jefe*,' Juan answered me with a telling grin. 'Maybe even some kind of private inquiry agent, much like . . . '

I nodded, trying to piece it all together. 'Stranger things have happened. Joseph Adler had been a heroin addict years ago, but got clean. He dabbled with cocaine, definitely dealt the drug, but seemed to give a lot of product away to friends and associates. Just a generous guy, perhaps?'

'Maybe he was using the drugs to buy access.'

I nodded, admitting that could be true. It seemed reasonable. 'Access to St. Simon?'

'Could be.'

'But why?'

'Who can say? Adler's dead. Not all things are knowable.'

I nodded. It made some kind of sense.

'Who else experimented with cocaine? Didn't Holmes himself use a seven percent solution to enliven his spirits when he had hit the skids? Maybe such a personality trait runs in the family. Maybe it's in the genes.'

I shrugged. I guessed anything was possible; but I had a more pertinent question to put to my young friend. 'If Adler was trying to buy access, or show he was a good earner as a drug dealer, who was he trying to impress?'

'You know?' Juan asked me.

'Okay, he wanted to get to St. Simon,' I said, stating the obvious, but then Juan expanded upon my theory.

'Yes, of course to get to St. Simon, but I think it was really to get to that gun. St. Simon must've told him about it. He wanted to get that gun. For that he needed to get close, and to do that he needed to be trusted. Joseph realized what that gun could mean, and he may have wanted to live up to his own heritage as a descendant of Sherlock Holmes and Irene Adler by solving an actual murder. A murder the police put down as unsolved — and maybe unsolvable.'

'Sounds nice,' I said, my voice dubious, 'but far-fetched, I think.'

'Maybe. But we know now that Holmes and Watson were real people, *Viejo*. We know Irene Adler was real; we can trace her back through Joseph Adler and his grandparents. His grandparents are old, but they verify his heritage. So why not Holmes and Watson also being real? Then why not Joseph Adler taking after his iconic ancestors?'

'It's an interesting theory, I'll give you that, Juan. But we're in a much more dangerous situation ourselves. No time for any more games. St. Simon's thugs tried to kill us, but they didn't succeed. They may try again.'

'Yes, they most certainly will, so we have to trap that fiend. Beat him at his own game,' Juan told me tersely. 'Like Holmes beat Moriarity.'

'I agree, but exactly how do we do that?'

'I have a plan, *Viejo*. Are you game?'

'You know I am, Juan.'

'Smashing, Watson!'

I looked at Juan and smiled hopelessly, then shrugged and proclaimed, 'Then the game's afoot, Holmes!'

16

Juan's Plan

'So what is it — this plan you have? And it better be good!' I demanded skeptically. It was the next morning, and Juan had met me at my apartment. I'd slept badly that night; he'd gone home early saying he had a few errands to run. I had no idea what possible errands he could have that late at night, but I was too tired to go into it with him just then. When he saw me that morning, he was smiling ear to ear.

He pulled out a .32 Beretta that was in a clear plastic Ziploc bag and handed it to me. I looked at him, aghast. 'Is this . . . ? You went to the police and took it back?'

Juan laughed good-naturedly. 'No, it's not *the* gun. But it's an exact duplicate of the .32 Beretta St. Simon used to murder my father.'

'That's interesting, I guess. But why?'

'Look, *Jefe*, ballistics tests will take a

few days, but we're running out of time. In the meantime, St. Simon hasn't been charged yet. Even if he is, he'll surely get bail. We still have some time, but we need to act fast. Immediately, actually. We can call him now, tell him we'll trade the gun for information on Joseph Adler's murder. He'll buy it, I'm sure. He's obsessed with getting that gun back. He didn't do Adler himself, but he had one of his men do it. I'm sure he'll sell that man out to us fast if he can get that gun back in trade.'

'That's your plan?' I looked at him incredulously. 'Where have you been? We just did a big press conference yesterday and gave the gun to the D.A. to reopen your father's murder case. It was all over the media.'

'Yes, and it had St. Simon so scared he had his boys throw a bomb through the window of your store to get rid of us. Revenge, most likely. But just suppose we tell him what we gave the cops was a fake, but we have the actual murder weapon if he still wants it?'

'He'll never buy that!' I shouted, thinking the whole idea was preposterous.

'He may or may not buy the story, but I'm sure his interest will be piqued by it. He may even *want* to believe it if we do this thing right,' Juan told me confidently. 'If we tell him we have that gun, he'll want it back because he *must* have it. We can meet with him and trade him the Beretta for the information we need.'

'And get killed,' I stated flatly.

'Perhaps.'

I looked at Juan. 'You really think he'll accept this story?'

'No, not really. But it just might get us in to see him, and that's what we really want. From that point on, we can find out what we need to know and act accordingly. You still have the phone number he gave us?'

I nodded.

'Good. Then you call him and talk to him. Tell him the gun and the press conference was just a way to get his attention. Let him know we're serious. Tell him the gun we gave the police was not the murder weapon; that we still have that gun, and he can still get it back if he's willing to pay.'

'Pay? You're going to ask for money from him for it?'

'Yes — not because we want or need the money, but because it's something he'll understand, being a criminal.'

I nodded slowly. 'You have a devious mind, my friend. All right, I think you might have something there.'

'St. Simon will bite. He'll have no choice. Curiosity will allow us to get in to see him. How we get out is anyone's guess, though.'

'So it's a kind of suicide mission.' I sighed grimly.

'Maybe, maybe not. I told you I have a plan.'

I looked at my young friend dubiously. I was 62 years old, and if we went through with this, it didn't look like I'd ever make it to 63. However, Juan was a lot younger than me, and he had a lot more to lose. If he was willing to go through with this, I couldn't back down in all good conscience. I looked at Juan skeptically. He smiled, knowing he had me onboard. I was a sucker for his crackpot scheme, and this one surely fitted the bill.

Juan looked at me carefully. 'Now, I want you to spruce up what you tell him a bit. Say we were holding out for more money — being a criminal, he'll understand that, maybe even appreciate it in his own twisted way. The price of doing business. He won't like it, but it'll ring true to him. That's all that's important. But part of our price will be the full dope on who did Joseph Adler and how. You insist he give that information to you. Don't back down on that demand. I don't think a guy like St. Simon would think twice about throwing one of his boys under the bus to save his own skin.'

'Yes, I guess that makes some kind of sense in his crooked world,' I said softly, sighing deeply, because just then I really figured that Juan was going to get us both killed.

'So you ready to do it?' he asked.

I looked at him, tense and thoughtful. 'Okay, that might get us in to see him, but what about when he finds out we tricked him? He may not notice the difference in the two guns by sight right off — after all, it's been a while since he's seen that particular .32 Beretta, and they all look pretty much alike — but he sure will know the serial number.'

'Maybe not. He might have to go check his files. I am sure he won't have it committed to memory. At least, I hope not. That might give us some time.'

'Time for what?' I asked nervously.

'Time for us to do what we have to do.'

I hoped Juan wasn't going all enigmatic on me again. I hated when he did that. I think he took being Holmes a bit too far sometimes. 'That's a big chance, Juan, and it doesn't give us much time to find out what we want to know before the roof falls in on us. I'm wondering how we get out of there alive afterwards.'

'Good question, Watson! I like that you're thinking ahead on this. It shows initiative.'

'I'm not kidding, Juan! Enough of that Watson crap. We could get killed in there. We *will* get killed! All St. Simon has to learn is that we tricked him and we're dead.'

'You're right, Prof, and I shouldn't be so flippant about such a dangerous situation. You want to back out? I can do it alone if you like.'

I sighed. 'No. We're in this together, to the end.'

'Bravo, Watson!'

'Juan, come on! Seriously, now — how do we get out and not end up dead? I'd really like to have some assurance of that before we go through with your hare-brained scheme.'

Juan shrugged, feigning that I had hurt his feelings with that hare-brained scheme talk. 'Nothing is certain in life, *Viejo*.'

Now he was becoming philosophical. 'Not what I want to hear. Try again, Juan!'

'Okay. When I left you last night, I went to see our two detective friends, Mallory and Johnson.'

'Them? Why? Don't tell me you think we can trust them now?'

'I don't know. I'm not totally sure. I also visited your friend Barry Zaruda, the D.A.'s brother. I set up something with them to have SWAT raid the St. Simon compound and set us free. See, by then, we'll surely have a serious hostage situation on our hands.'

'A hostage situation!' I blurted fearfully. I'd not thought of that. 'What do you mean?'

'Well, that could happen — I mean if St. Simon doesn't kill us outright, of course, which I admit is a good possibility. I see that as a more than likely odds-on favorite reaction from him. However, he'll also be so crazy angry when he realizes we tricked him, he may keep us alive . . . You know, for torture . . .

'Torture!' I shouted. This was sounding worse by the minute.

'Of course. He'll be furious with us. So he might keep us alive a bit longer, you know, to torture us later. At least I hope so. That's good.'

'You hope so? That's good?' I asked dubiously, nervous and totally confused now. But I noted Juan was entirely serious and even smiling.

'Yes — good in the sense that becoming a hostage is better than being killed instantly. Don't you agree? If we're being held hostage, we're still alive. See what I mean? As long as there's life, there's hope. It also gives the cops the excuse they've waited for to get into St. Simon's fortress estate and see just what he's been up to. They'll have search warrants for all his records and computers, confiscate his gun collection, and process his thug guards, of which most I'm sure are carrying illegally, and may even have their own warrants outstanding. Anyway, those AKs and other heavy-duty weapons we saw his guards carrying are certainly not legal, so there's plenty of things for the cops, FBI, and the ATF to discover there. Once they can legally gain access. They'll be busy for some time, but the main thing is that the raid will cause all kinds of commotion and give us the diversion we need — and some time — to get safe. I hope.'

'You're taking a big chance, Juan.'

'*We're* taking a big chance, *Viejo*. But it's worth it, don't you think? To find out who murdered Joseph Adler, and to take down St. Simon, it's worth it.'

I nodded. 'Okay, let's do it. I'll make the call.'

'Just one thing, *Jefe*,' he said with a mischievous smile.

'Yes . . . Juan?' I looked at him with growing trepidation.

'I also want you to take the lead when we meet with St. Simon when it comes to talking. You do the negotiating when we get in to see him. You're the Professor, and older, so presumably wiser and more experienced.'

'Presumably? Well, thank you, I think.'

Juan smiled at me, then continued, 'Our case would work better coming from you. And besides I have a few tricks up my sleeve, so I need to be . . . unencumbered.'

The lead? Me? I just shook my head dubiously and looked at my young friend as the impact of the rest of his statement hit me. 'And exactly what tricks are you talking about, Juan? Tell me!'

'Not now. You just make the call first, set up the meeting, and tell him we'll come out to his house with the right gun, ready to deal. Tell him that what he saw with the cops on TV and the news was all a show to get his attention and we didn't give them the correct gun. It'll come out soon enough that it was some kind of hoax. Tell him we still have the gun he wants and that we're willing to deal. Now make the case.'

'He'll never believe that, Juan!'

'No, but he'll *want* to believe it, and a supreme egotist like him can never pass up the chance to find out. *Make* him believe it!'

'You know, you have a devious criminal mind, my friend.'

'Good genes, I guess, *Viejo*.'

17

Ready to Deal

The meeting was set up for later that afternoon at Charles St. Simon's walled and guarded estate in the East Side war zone. I made the call and set up the parameters. Juan and I would come out to him to close the deal, and we'd bring the gun with us — the gun that he wanted now more than anything in the world. We were taking a big chance. It was a bogus gun, but he didn't know that. Not yet.

My old Chevy was gone, blown away in the blast that had destroyed my bookstore — which was something I was not forgetting. St. Simon knew I didn't have a car any longer, so he offered to have one of his men drive out and pick us up in his own personal limo. That did not sit well with me, but I had no choice but to accept the offer. He insisted, actually, making it a part of the deal.

Juan and I did not speak one word on the long drive through Dorchester over to the East River, over the bridge and into the East Side war zone that St. Simon had created through his drug dealing. It was the part of our city he ruled like it was his own private country.

I sighed, looking over at Juan nervously as we pulled up to St. Simon's walled estate. Our brilliant plan was a much more nerve-wracking prospect now that we were there, entering the belly of the beast. I was terrified, and had a real effort keeping myself calm and focused. I saw the lead thug, Reggie, the guy with the missing thumb and forefinger, whom I remembered from our previous visit. He was on guard duty with an assortment of other nasty-looking thugs.

He recognized us and motioned us out of the car and over to him and his men. The one good thing was that they had been told to expect us, and to take us to the house to see the boss right away. They had us checked for weapons most carefully. I held out the bag to him. 'This is what we brought for Mr. St. Simon.'

'I know all about that,' Reggie growled, grabbed it, opened it, looked inside and saw the .32 Beretta in the clear plastic Ziploc bag and nodded. He gave us a death's head smile. I was sure that he never expected to see us alive again this side of hell. It did nothing to improve my confidence in Juan's plan. I looked at Juan and he just smiled back casually, as if we were merely taking a jaunt to his granny's house.

Reggie waved us forward. 'Follow Humphrey up to the house. Mr. St. Simon is expecting you. And this.'

I nodded, Juan and I following our armed escort in a slow walk to the boss-man's big house. There were six of them and they had us covered with weapons every foot of the way. Humphrey held the bag with the Beretta in it as carefully as if it were a newborn baby. Once we reached the big house, Humphrey turned us over to Ahmad and his housebound goon squad. They checked us again for weapons. Humphrey then gave Ahmad the bag with the Beretta in it, and then he and his men left.

Now we were inside the house — halfway to our goal.

Ahmad and his men led us through the house into the back garden room, where we had met with St. Simon before. The sun was low in the sky this time; it was later afternoon, and the large room was just as I remembered it, with huge picture windows that let in the light and heat. There were plants and flowers everywhere, and the same white table and chairs in the center of the room. It seemed like such a nice place to relax, maybe do some reading in peace and quiet, so I wondered why I was unable to relax at all. Impending doom, most likely.

Ahmad walked us over to the table and told us to sit. We sat. He then stood off to the side, waiting. We all waited. I noticed that in one hand the thug held the bag with the Beretta, while in the other a .45 auto was pointed directly at us.

We waited silently for the big man to appear, none of us saying a word. There was nothing to say at that point anyway.

Suddenly the fancy white French doors at the far end of the room burst open and

Charles St. Simon entered. He looked the same as he had when we had met him days before: tall, lean, a rather muscular black man with a bald pate and eyes that glowed like a snake. His mouth had gleaming white teeth, but when he smiled it still reminded me of a shark ready to devour its prey.

That would be us. I swallowed hard, my throat dry as parchment and feeling like it was closing in upon me. Terror does that to you.

St. Simon strode over to us and leered down at us defiantly. 'So you came back and you've brought me the gun as I asked,' he said, coming closer, showing me his shark teeth. It was then that a dark feeling of doom overcame me, and I knew for certain we were dead men and never getting out of there alive.

I sighed sadly, knowing now that we were defeated. We'd have to go through with our plan and play the cards we had been dealt — play them through to the end. I had to be brave. There was nothing else to do now.

Juan nudged me, giving me my cue to

start my rap. I swallowed nervously, tried to focus, and began firmly: 'We have a deal. We've delivered our part of it as we agreed. We don't care about the additional money. We'll not inconvenience you with that. We'll trade you the gun in exchange for the name of the person who murdered Joseph Adler and evidence on how he did it.'

St. Simon smiled broadly at his good fortune at having us and the gun delivered into his hands so easily, so effortlessly. He nodded tersely. 'Ahmad, will you do me a small favor, please?'

'Yes, sir.'

'Take your .45 and place one slug each into the foreheads of each of these men.'

'Yes, sir,' Ahmad replied firmly. I had no doubt at all that he would carry out his murderous order.

Juan and I froze like deer in headlights. I had feared this, of course; but the fact that it actually was going to happen had me shocked to the core of my being. I was going to die. Juan was going to die. We were going to be shot dead!

I watched as Ahmad dutifully took aim

at my head, and I almost fainted. Then I heard Juan quickly speak up for the first time, coldly serious, almost threateningly: 'I wouldn't do that *yet*, Mr. St. Simon.'

The drug kingpin's eyes riveted to Juan like a cobra about to spring. 'And why not?'

'Because you have *a* gun, but you still don't have *the* gun,' Juan said simply.

Charles St. Simon held up his hand to stop Ahmad and the thug lowered his weapon. The smile left St. Simon's face, replaced by anger as he grabbed the bag out of Ahmad's hand, upending the contents onto the table in front of us. Out fell the .32 Beretta from its clear plastic Ziploc bag that was *not* St. Simon's gun, and a letter.

I took a deep breath for the first time in many moments. What was Juan doing? Was he crazy? He was giving our game away!

St. Simon looked at the gun suspiciously, took it from the table, lifted it up, and looked it over carefully, curiously, uncertainly. Then he placed it back in the plastic bag and lay it on the table. He looked at us with fire in his eyes.

Then Juan really let the cat out of the bag. 'Of course, that's a very nice .32 Beretta, but it isn't *the* Beretta that you seek, Mr. St. Simon. *That* particular gun is safely hidden in a place where, I assure you, you'll never find it. It'll go straight to the D.A. if anything happens to us. Like if we're unable to leave your house in the next half hour and report to the police that we're safe and unharmed. The gun we gave the D.A., the gun the news media reported, was another .32, also not *your* gun.'

St. Simon gave us a cold reptilian *I-promise-I-will-kill-you* look, but he only said, 'I see.'

Juan nudged me again. I collected my thoughts and tamped down my fear with a Herculean effort. 'Ah yes, so do we still have a deal? You can still get the actual gun that you want. We have it. All you have to do is give up the killer of Joseph Adler and guarantee us safe passage out of here.'

St. Simon glared at me, then smiled tightly, giving me an *I-can-always-have-you-killed-later* look. I swallowed hard, knowing he wasn't kidding about that, and he could easily make it happen. Hadn't he almost killed us when he'd had my store bombed?

'Who killed Joseph Adler? It was on your order, wasn't it?' I asked the criminal kingpin.

Charles St. Simon thought about that for a moment, then looked over at his lieutenant, Ahmad. 'Please leave the room; I want to be alone with these men. Give me your .45 before you go.'

Ahmad dutifully handed over his .45 to St. Simon, which the gangster immediately pointed right at me.

'Now, gentlemen, let's stop this foolishness and get down to business,' St. Simon offered, his mouth twisted into a dark snarl. He was doing his best to hold his vicious anger in check, and I hoped he would be successful.

I nodded. 'I told you the only thing we want. You heard my questions. Do you want me to repeat them?' I asked, trying to keep my teeth from chattering and wondering why Juan was so silent.

'No, but that was a neat trick bringing

in a bogus gun, and then that story about the real one. That took real guts. I may have that written on your tombstones. Now I don't know what to believe. In fact, I don't think I believe you at all now.'

'Oh, you'd better believe me,' I said. 'We have your Beretta and a signed letter from Joseph Adler about the gun and the Alberto Marcano murder. A murder from many years ago, early in your career, and the killing of my friend's father. Tell us what we want to know and you'll get what you want.'

St. Simon's face flashed blind red rage, and for a second I thought he was personally going to shoot Juan and me right then and there. Kill us stone cold dead. Then he suddenly shrugged. 'It's of no consequence. The truth? You won't believe the truth, but I'll tell you anyway. No, I didn't kill Joseph Adler, or order him to be killed. In truth, I liked that kid. I brought him up and taught him the business. I was grooming him to take over operations on the West Side. He was young, smart, and best of all, white. He could go places and get into places I could never go — I had a rep in certain circles, you see, and he didn't. Not then. I was the one who got him off the heroin, got him into distributing it for me, also later cocaine. He was very good. Maybe too good. Some of my people became jealous.'

'Who did the deed?' I demanded.

'My man Reggie did it, all on his own. He and two other morons took Adler down in that house on the West Side — the house you're always trying to get closed.' His eyes shot daggers over at Juan. 'It's my house. Reggie took Bill and Shorty with him to do it. They'll talk. They'll spill. They held Adler down, then Reggie gave him the hot shot that killed him. Gave him the OD.'

This didn't seem to make sense to me. I was surprised, wondering what the real deal was, and asked, 'I don't think I buy it! Reggie is still alive; he still works for you. We just saw him at the gate. Why is he still alive, if he did the Adler killing against your orders?'

'It all happened so fast. At the same time that I discovered my Beretta was missing from my gun collection in the other room — a collection I prided myself on, and had shown to Joseph one time when I invited him here — he stole the gun. It all happened just as Reggie decided to act on his own to eliminate a rival. I trusted Joseph! I liked that kid! But then he turned on me!' St. Simon growled, enraged. 'I did not deserve that betrayal!'

We were quiet for a long moment. St. Simon actually looked as if his feelings were hurt. I looked to Juan, hoping he would add something to help me out, but he was silent.

'What about Reggie?' I demanded.

St. Simon calmed down and looked at me seriously. 'The two events happened at the same time, almost the same instant. I only then realized that Joseph stole the Beretta. He was the only person who knew about it. He was the only person who could have taken it. It was one of my earliest collectable guns, but it held a secret. It was the only gun I had ever used in an actual murder. My first and only personal murder. It could connect me to the Alberto Marcano murder — to your fathe . . . ' He looked hard at Juan, and Juan just glared back at him defiantly. Neither man said another word, and I had no idea what they were thinking or going to do next, but I could see their faces twisted in what looked to me to be less than an inch away from pure unadulterated hatred.

I noticed St. Simon's finger twitching on the trigger of the .45, waiting for Juan to make his move. I stared at my young friend, reaching my hand out to his arm to hold him back from rushing headlong at the man who had murdered his father — and would surely murder him in cold blood were he to make a move. Juan was, after all, unarmed. The tension peaked fearfully and then ebbed. We all took a deep breath.

'Please continue, Mr. St. Simon. What happened next?' I asked, trying to move things along and away from utter catastrophe for the two of us.

'Well, I sent my people out looking for Joseph and the missing gun, naturally. When I heard what Reggie had done, on his own and not on my order, I was angry with him, certainly, but . . . You'll notice Reggie is missing the thumb and forefinger on his right hand?'

'Yes, I saw that,' I replied, remembering his bandaged hand.

'Those were the offensive digits that gave Joseph Adler his hot shot, against my orders. So I had them removed. Reggie was very upset about it, but he'd disobeyed me by acting on his own without my orders. I can't allow that. But, as it turns out, his instincts proved far better than my own in that one situation. I couldn't kill such an able employee, but he had to pay a price for his action to set an example to my people. He did. It's over with now.'

I nodded. So Reggie committed the murder, and we could get this Bill and Shorty to testify. That was something. The Joseph Adler case seemed solved. Now all Juan and I had to do was get the hell out of there alive long enough to get the information to the police.

I grew grim. 'And you had my store bombed?'

'Yes, to teach you a lesson. But you haven't been harmed, so don't make so much out of it now. After all, only a few old books were damaged,' St. Simon stated in an offhand manner.

I wanted to strangle him then and there. Juan looked at me with alarm, but I was fuming. 'Damaged? Everything was totally destroyed!' I barked, seeing red now. 'Thousands of my books are gone! Wonderful, priceless books — my entire store. Lost forever!'

'They are just books, after all. What you have to be happy about is the fact that you're both still alive,' the gangster leader said. 'Accept that. For now.'

'Just books!' I growled defiantly, unable to get the rage I felt out of my craw; but I could see that Juan was concerned by my outburst. After all, I was supposed to be his Watson — I was a professor and therefore the stable, calm one in our partnership.

St. Simon smiled evilly, pointing his .45 at me with pleasure. Waiting.

'*Jefe!* Calm down!' Juan told me sternly, holding me in check with his words. 'Focus! Focus!'

I nodded, hot and angry, forgetting for a moment how scared I was and how much danger we were in.

St. Simon leered at me. 'Now I need the location of the real gun, if you in fact have it. Or I'll just shoot you both dead here and now. How does that sound?'

'We did find the murder weapon, and a letter written and signed by Joseph Adler,' I said slowly and carefully, as St. Simon's eyes bored into my own, while I saw Juan silently move away from me. 'But I have to tell you the truth — I lied to you before. That weapon's been delivered as evidence to D.A. Zaruda and is now being tested for — '

St. Simon's face grew beet-red with rage and the knowledge that he had been tricked once again. He lifted the .45 in an attempt to point and squeeze off a slug at me just as Juan grabbed up the bag on the table. Everything then happened so fast. Suddenly Juan aimed the .32 in the bag and somehow got off two shots through the bag into St. Simon. It happened just as the gangster got off a shot at me. I can't imagine how Juan's finger found the trigger through the bag to get off two shots. I was also astonished to learn that the Beretta had been loaded all along! I looked at my young partner and realized that there was quite a bit more to him than met the eye.

The utter confusion and loud shots had my head spinning in terror. I felt a sharp pain in my arm. Then, in an instant, it was over. Charles St. Simon was lying on the floor bleeding from the chest; the .45 had dropped from his hand. His slug from that .45 had found me, but it had only grazed my arm, thankfully. I was bleeding a bit; but considering the situation, I knew I had gotten off very lucky in that shootout, and was not complaining. Though my wound hurt like hell.

'You never told me that Beretta was loaded!' I shouted at Juan, aghast. 'I had no idea!'

'It's better you didn't know. Anyway, you just assumed like everyone else that it *wasn't* loaded, right?'

'Of course!' I admitted. That was

obvious. 'Who the hell would bring a loaded gun to a — '

'Well, so did St. Simon and his guards. I figured I'd take the chance, and it proved to be my ace in the hole, *Viejo*,' Juan stated triumphantly.

'You're quite amazing,' I said with genuine admiration. 'You acted quick, just like — '

'Holmes?' he asked me with a wry grin.

'Yes, just like Sherlock Holmes . . . '

'As you did also, good old Watson,' Juan replied with a wink.

I shook my head and rolled my eyes at him. Then I lifted my shirt to wipe the blood trickling from my wound. Thankfully, it was only superficial. I didn't even have to faint. I looked at St. Simon bleeding out upon the floor, moaning in pain from wounds that were much more serious. Juan came over to me and placed the Beretta in my hand as he grabbed up the .45 from the floor.

'What's going on?' I blurted.

'The door.'

I looked up, wondering just what he was talking about, when I saw my young companion point his .45 towards the French doors at the other end of the room. Suddenly there was a massive commotion outside and all around the house. I heard gun shots. I knew the SWAT raid was now in progress; their cue had been the gunshots coming from inside the house.

Suddenly there was noise and chaos all around the house and grounds. Screaming. Yells. More gun shots. Juan still kept careful aim at the door, and soon it opened and Ahmad entered. He was not carrying his .45 — he'd given that to St. Simon; now Juan had it and was aiming the man's own gun at him. But instead, Ahmad held an AK47 and seemed ready to use it on us. Juan fired off three quick rounds that shattered the door around him and Ahmad quickly left the room. He did not come back. There was more gunfire from other areas inside the house now, from other rooms, and from all around the grounds outside. We stayed where we were, guns out and ready.

Juan helped me up and we checked on St. Simon. He wasn't dead, but he would soon be if he didn't get help right away.

He was bleeding badly.

'I'll go get help,' I offered, but Juan grabbed me and held me back forcefully.

'No, *Viejo*, let him die. Here and now. It is his life or ours. If he lives, we're dead men. There's no other way. I'm sorry, but we can't save him.'

I looked at my young friend and felt a sadness at his cold pragmatism, something I'd never felt in me before, because I hated what he was saying, but I realized he was right — we had no choice. At that moment, I even feared Juan himself might put another slug, a .45 this time, into St. Simon to end the gangster's life once and for all before EMS came. I hoped that would not happen. Aside from the moral issue, it might result in some complicated questions we didn't need from the police. Thankfully, Juan didn't do it. We just stood there, a somber death watch as chaos and gunfire went on all around us throughout the house. Then it stopped as suddenly as it had begun.

18

Case Closed

I looked at Juan and he looked at me and just shrugged. We waited. We did not have long to wait. A minute or so later Detectives Mallory and Johnson entered the room.

'You two okay?' Mallory asked us gruffly.

'Yeah, but St. Simon needs a doctor,' I stated.

Juan looked at me reproachfully. He shook his head in disagreement with my words.

Mallory came over, looked at Charles St. Simon, and bent down and took his pulse. 'I don't think so. Not any longer. This one's dead.'

We handed Mallory and Johnson the hardware — my .32 Beretta and Juan's .45 — and then told them what St. Simon had told us about the murder of Joseph Adler.

'So it was a hot shot! I'll be damned!' Mallory said.

'We told you,' I said, trying not to be too sarcastic.

'Okay, so you told us. You think we believe everything people tell us? Forget about it! But no problem, we'll get it all sorted out now. We have Reggie, he's being held with the rest of St. Simon's crew. We'll get Bill and Shorty to roll over on him, and that will close that case very nicely. We're all about closing cases,' Johnson stated with a wide grin. It was the first time I ever saw anything even approaching a smile from the man.

'Yeah,' I retorted. 'Just close them the right way from now on.'

Mallory nodded. 'Sorry, we really were trying to keep you guys out of something we knew you couldn't handle.'

'Well, we seemed to have handled it pretty damn well,' Juan said.

'You were very lucky,' Mallory told us with brash sincerity. I knew he was correct.

I looked over at Juan, then to Mallory, and said, 'Well next time . . . Ah, what I mean to say is, thanks for being here when we needed you.'

'No problem,' Mallory answered, allowing a slight grin. 'Actually, you guys did good. We're proud of you both.'

* * *

It was six weeks later when a new bookstore in Dorchester opened its doors to the public. My insurance payment, augmented by a significant collection put up for sale, had made it all possible. The media notoriety from the closing of the Alberto Marcano cold case and the Joseph Adler murder presented Juan and myself with some measure of publicity. We used it to promote the new bookstore.

That new store was now called Jones & Marcano — Rare Books, and we had a great selection of collectable and rare first editions, modern firsts, and even some classic vintage paperbacks. We'd stripped my apartment bare of books, then took down the shelves and relocated them to the store. Then we filled all the shelves of the store with all of my best books. The store looked great, and it had a most impressive stock now. We had customers coming from all over to buy our books.

My young partner, Juan Marcano, was also getting into the 'book thing' as he called it, learning about first editions, points, values, and so on. I taught him well. We were successful and things were looking up. I still had that copy of *The Strand Magazine* and the torn page from that mysterious diary or notebook. It was now sealed in protective Lucite plastic and on display in the store as a page from the secret diary of Dr. John H. Watson given to us by Joseph Adler, the great-grandson of Sherlock Holmes and Irene Adler. We never forgot it, or him! But there was still one nagging question. Where was the rest of Watson's diary?

'We make a good team, Juan,' I told my young friend that evening as we were closing up for the day. Sales that day had been brisk. It was a situation I had never been used to in the old store, but this new store was different. I think it was all because of Juan. He had a certain winning way with people.

‘Yes, we do make a good team, *Viejo*,’ Juan replied with a grin.

‘I’m also glad we’re partners in the new store.’

‘I’m glad you took me in.’

‘I’ll make a first-class bookman out of you yet.’

‘I’m here to learn, *Jefe*.’

‘That’s good, Juan. And while we’re selling books, I was thinking . . . ’

‘Always a bad sign, *Viejo*,’ Juan told me, laughing with a twinge of nervousness, ‘but tell me anyway. What were you thinking?’

‘You know.’

Juan just smiled, got up from his seat and walked over to the safe and pulled out the battered old tin dispatch box that we both believed to have once belonged to Sherlock Holmes’s friend and companion, Dr. John H. Watson. ‘There’s this,’ Juan said, placing the box firmly down in front of me. The .32 Beretta and Joseph Adler’s letter were still in the hands of the police as evidence. Now only the tin box sat before us, empty — and that was the question and the mystery.

I looked at my young partner carefully and inquired, 'Yes?'

'We still have a case here that needs to be solved. We need to find the contents of Watson's old dispatch box. We need to find that diary.'

I sighed. He was correct. Out of all the things we'd accomplished, we never solved the original case that we'd set out to solve — finding the rest of that diary. But where? How? Juan was getting rambunctious again. I knew what that meant, but I could not help but smile at my young friend. 'All right then, I agree. But I want us to investigate this case just like Holmes and Watson would.'

'Yes, just like Sherlock Holmes and Dr. Watson would do it, eh, *Watson*?' Juan answered, showing me his mischievous smile.

I sighed and nodded. I could play along, 'Sure, Holmes. The game seems to be afoot once again. We need to locate Watson's diary. So where do we begin?'

'Why, at the beginning, of course.' And he held up the battered old dispatch box in front of me, tipped it upside down and revealed a false bottom that held one lone piece of paper.

'Juan! What is it?' I asked, astonished. 'How did you know it was there?'

'One thing at a time, *Viejo*,' Juan told me as he carefully unfolded the paper and set it down on the counter in front of me.

'Why . . . ? Is that a map?'

'Very good, *Viejo*. Yes, it's a map — but not just any map, I'll venture. It's a treasure map. A map that'll lead us to Watson's secret papers — his treasure.'

'How?' I blurted in astonishment. 'How did you discover this?'

'I noticed the hidden compartment when I examined underneath the box this morning. I noticed a slim sleeve of tin, and when I wedged it open I found this small piece of paper tucked inside — the map,' Juan said simply.

'Amazing! Simply amazing!' I stammered in awe. 'This changes everything!'

'Indeed it does. So, are you with me?'

I nodded in pure excitement. 'You know that I am.'

'Good, then we continue our partnership. One case has been closed successfully, and tomorrow we begin another. Is that all right with you?'

'Yes!' I blurted, full of enthusiasm. 'Of course!'

'Of course — *what*?' he asked me playfully.

I sighed, looking at his big smiling face. 'Okay, if I must?'

'You must.'

I took a deep breath. 'Well then, of course . . . Holmes!'

'That's it, Watson! I'll make an ace detective out of you yet!'

'Hah! And I'll make a first-rate bookman out of you before all this is over and done, my young friend.'

'That's a deal, *Viejo*!'

Other titles in the
Linford Mystery Library:

THE LIBRARY DETECTIVE RETURNS

James Holding

Former Homicide cop Hal Johnson now works as 'library fuzz' — spending his days chasing down overdue books, stolen volumes, and owed fines. He doesn't miss life in the fast lane. But his police training and detective instincts still prove necessary in the bibliographic delinquency division. For such apparently innocuous peccadillos on the part of borrowers often set Hal on the trail towards uncovering greater crimes: fraud, theft, drug-smuggling, arson — and even murder . . .

THE GRIM JOKER

Gerald Verner

Mr. Hamilton Lorne is amused to receive a card with the grotesque picture of a fool, complete with cap and bells, one finger pointing at the holder. He and Superintendent Budd of Scotland Yard laugh at the threatening limerick scrawled across the back, assuming it is a feeble practical joke, and drop the card into a waste-paper basket. But no one is laughing when the following morning Mr. Lorne is found dead, stabbed through the heart — the first in a series of sadistic murders perpetrated by the elusive Grim Joker.

DEAD MAN'S PAIN

Valerie Holmes

A man being pursued collides with Nicholas Penn. Assuming his pocket has been pilfered in the scuffle, Nicholas also gives chase. But the stranger fails to see a horse careering down the road, and is trampled by the animal, seemingly mortally. Later, though, Nicholas discovers that the man was no thief — and still lives. Mystified, he is determined to discover the truth behind the 'dead' man's pain . . .

MORE SECRET FILES OF SHERLOCK HOLMES

Gary Lovisi

Five untold tales of the great detective. In the first, Holmes chronicles to Watson a strange event at a freak show years before he met the good doctor. The second sees Watson throwing a birthday party for his friend — but danger lurks among the festivities. The detective and the doctor play golf at St. Andrews, and then are invited to Paris to solve a most perplexing art theft. Finally, Conan Doyle's Professor Challenger meets the duo, who arrive in the hope of preventing an attempt on his life.

THE HUNTSMAN

Gerald Verner

Superintendent Budd is faced with one of his toughest assignments in separating the strands of mystery that grip the village of Chalebury: a series of robberies perpetrated by the burglar known as Stocking-foot; sightings of the ghostly Huntsman; and the murders of a villager and a local police inspector. Interweaving with these is the suspicious behaviour of a frightened young woman who lives in a large dilapidated house with one elderly servant. Is there a connection between all these crimes and other oddities happening in the tiny village?